**"This cottage and the land it stands on have been in my family for generations, and I have no wish to sell," Dante continued, breaking through her defeated thoughts. "But I am prepared to give Orla half the value. Fifty-fifty."**

Aislin covered her mouth with a trembling hand. "Thank you. You don't know what that means..."

"I also have an offer for you," he cut in before she could get carried away.

"What kind of offer?"

"A mutually beneficial one." His eyes narrowed and he rocked his head forward as if he were thinking. Then he gave one final nod and stilled. "I have a wedding to attend this weekend. I want you to come with me."

"You want me to come to a wedding with you?"

"*Sí.* And in return I will pay you one million euros."

## Conveniently Wed!

*Conveniently wedded, passionately bedded!*

Whether there's a debt to be paid, a will to be obeyed or a business to be saved...she's got no choice but to say, "I do!"

But these billionaire bridegrooms have got another think coming if they imagine marriage will be that easy...

Soon their convenient brides become the objects of inconvenient desire!

Find out what happens after the vows in:

*The Greek's Bought Bride* by Sharon Kendrick

*Claiming His Wedding Night Consequence* by Abby Green

*Bound by a One-Night Vow* by Melanie Milburne

*Sicilian's Bride for a Price* by Tara Pammi

*Claiming His Christmas Wife* by Dani Collins

*My Bought Virgin Wife* by Caitlin Crews

Look for more Conveniently Wed! coming soon!

*Michelle Smart*

# THE SICILIAN'S BOUGHT CINDERELLA



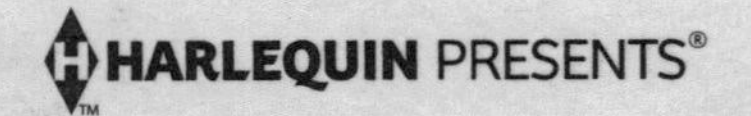

Recycling programs for this product may not exist in your area.

ISBN-13: 978-1-335-47805-4

The Sicilian's Bought Cinderella

First North American publication 2019



This edition published by arrangement with Harlequin Books S.A.

For questions and comments about the quality of this book, please contact us at CustomerService@Harlequin.com.

**Printed in U.S.A.**

**Michelle Smart**'s love affair with books started when she was a baby, when she would cuddle them in her cot. A voracious reader of all genres, she found her love of romance established when she stumbled across her first Harlequin book at the age of twelve. She's been reading—and writing—them ever since. Michelle lives in Northamptonshire, England, with her husband and two young Smarties.

**Books by Michelle Smart**

**Harlequin Presents**

*Once a Moretti Wife*
*A Bride at His Bidding*

***One Night With Consequences***

*Claiming His Christmas Consequence*

***Wedlocked!***

*Wedded, Bedded, Betrayed*

***Bound to a Billionaire***

*Protecting His Defiant Innocent*
*Claiming His One-Night Baby*
*Buying His Bride of Convenience*

***Rings of Vengeance***

*Billionaire's Bride for Revenge*
*Marriage Made in Blackmail*
*Billionaire's Baby of Redemption*

Visit the Author Profile page at Harlequin.com for more titles.

To all the Emmas in my life. Love you all! Xxx

# CHAPTER ONE

DANTE MONCADA JUMPED into the car beside his driver, two of his men clambering in behind him. This was all he needed, someone breaking into the old cottage that had been in the Moncada family's possession for generations.

As his driver navigated Palermo's narrow streets and headed into the rolling countryside, Dante thought back to his earlier conversation with Riccardo D'Amore. The head of the D'Amore family had put the brakes on a deal Dante had been negotiating for the past six months. Riccardo ran a clean, wholesome business and was concerned Dante's reputation would tarnish it.

He muttered a curse under his breath and resisted the urge to punch the dashboard.

What reputation? So he liked the ladies. That was no crime. His business empire was built on legitimate money. He did not play the games many Sicilian men liked to play. He kept his nose clean literally and figuratively. He liked to drink and party, but so what? He didn't touch drugs, never gambled and avoided the circles where arms, drug dealing and people trafficking were considered profitable business enterprises. He worked hard. Building a multi-billion-euro technology empire from a modest million-euro inheritance, and with an accountancy trail even the most hardened auditor would fail to find fault with, took dedication. For sure, he cut the odd corner here and there, and his Sicilian heritage meant he did not suffer fools, but every cent he'd earned he'd earned legitimately.

But the legitimacy of his business was not the factor behind Riccardo's foot coming down on the deal that Dante and Alessio, Riccardo's eldest son, had spent months working on. The D'Amores had developed the next-generation safety system for smartphones that had proven itself hack-proof, out-performing all rivals. Alessio and Dante were all set to sign an exclusivity agreement for Dante to install the system in the smartphones and tablets his company was Europe's leader in. This system would give him the tools to penetrate America, the only continent Dante was still to get a decent foothold in.

Riccardo's talk about reputations boiled down to one thing. Dante's parentage. His recently deceased father, Salvatore, had been a heavy gambler and the ultimate playboy. His mother, Immacolata, was known unaffectionately as the Black Widow, a moniker Dante had always thought unfair, as she had never actually killed any of her husbands, merely leeched them for money when she divorced them. His father had been her first husband. She was currently on number five. His mother lived like a queen.

Riccardo, on the other hand, had had one wife, eleven children, thought gambling the work of the devil and sex outside the confines of marriage a sin. Riccardo was concerned Dante was the apple that hadn't fallen far from the tree. Riccardo wanted proof that Dante was not the mere sum of his parents' parts and would not bring Amore Systems and by extension Riccardo himself into disrepute. Riccardo was now in advanced talks with Dante's biggest rival about contracting the system to them instead.

Damn him. The old fool was supposed to have retired.

He had one chance to prove his respectability before the deal was lost for good, Alessio's forthcoming wedding.

Dante's angry ruminations on his business problems were put to one side when his driver pulled the car to a stop in a small opening amidst the dense woodland that ran along the driveway to the cottage. A few metres away, also cunningly hidden in the woodland, was a much smaller city car…

Dante reached into the footwell for the baseball bat he hoped he wouldn't have to use.

Flanked by his bodyguards, he neared the rundown farmer's cottage through the thick trees that hid their approach from watching eyes and rubbed his arms against the bracing chill under the cloudless night sky. The remnants of what had been an unusually cold winter still lingered in the air.

The small cottage with its peeling whitewashed exterior walls came into view. All the shutters were closed but smoke curled out of the chimney that hadn't been used in two decades, wisping upwards into the still darkness of this early spring Sicilian evening. Marcello, who managed the land, had been correct that someone was there.

Keeping to the shadows, Dante and his men approached it.

The door was locked.

Brow furrowing, he pulled his key out and unlocked it.

He winced as the sounds of the creaking hinges echoed through the walls, and stepped inside for the first time since his teenage years, when he would sneak girls there. It hadn't been his father he'd worried about catching him, it had been the girls' fathers. Sicilian men did not take kindly to their daughters having a sex life before marriage; at least, they hadn't twenty years ago.

The open-plan interior was much smaller than he remembered. The lights already on, he scanned it quickly, looking for damage. The window above the sink had been boarded in cardboard. He guessed that was where the intruder had gained entry, but there was no other visible damage, nothing to suggest his unwelcome visitor had come here intent on vandalising or robbing them. Not that there was anything to take unless the intruder had a penchant for decades-old musty furniture. An air of neglect permeated the walls, mingling with the black smoke billowing from the log fire. A pile of what looked like educational books was stacked on the small table.

He stared at those books, brow furrowed again at their incongruity.

A floorboard creaked above his head.

Adrenaline surged through him.

Keeping a tight hold on the baseball bat, Dante nodded at his men to follow and treaded slowly up the narrow staircase, cursing that each step was received with yet another creak. He could have left his men to deal with the intruder but he wanted to see the face of the man who'd had the nerve to break into his property before deciding what to do with him.

Like all men with his wealth and power, Dante had enemies. The question he asked himself was if it was one of those enemies hiding behind this door plotting against him or just a cold vagrant chancing his luck.

He nodded at his men one more time and pushed the door open.

His first thought as he entered the empty bedroom was that he was too late and the intruder had escaped. There was no second thought, for a figure suddenly burst through from the *en suite* bathroom and charged at him, screaming, with what looked like a showerhead in hand.

It took a long beat before his brain recognised the screeching figure for what it was—a woman.

Before the showerhead in her hand could connect with Dante's head, Lino, the quicker of his men, grabbed hold of the woman and engulfed her in his meaty arms.

Immediately she started kicking out, hurling a string of obscenities in what sounded like English, but with a strong accent he had trouble placing.

Dante stared with amazement at this struggling intruder dressed only in a thick maroon robe.

Her eyes fell on him. There was a wild terror in the returning stare.

'Let her go,' he ordered.

Lino removed the showerhead from her hand and released her.

As soon as she was free from his hold, she backed away from them, her eyes going from Dante, to Lino, to Vincenzo and back to Dante, the terror still there.

He quite understood her fear. Dante was tall and physically imposing. Lino and Vincenzo were mountains.

'Leave,' he barked at his men. 'Wait downstairs for me.'

Her eyes settled on him.

This woman might be an intruder, her reasons for being there to be revealed but, unless she had a gun hiding beneath that robe, which she would have already used if she'd had one, she posed no danger.

His men were too well trained to argue and left the room. Stealth no longer being needed, they thumped down the stairs like a herd of wildebeest.

Now that he was alone with her, Dante's senses became more attuned. A wonderful scent filled the room, a soft floral smell that clung around the intruder, who had backed herself into the corner of the room. The only sound to be heard was her ragged breathing.

He stepped slowly towards her.

She pressed herself more tightly into the corner of the room and hugged her arms across her seemingly ample chest, strikingly angled eyes ringing with fear at him. If she hadn't broken into his property and made herself at home, he could feel sorry for her.

He guessed her to be in her early twenties, petite yet curvy, snub nose, plump lips, freckles covering a face that was either naturally pale or white from fright. The colour of her long, wet hair was impossible to judge. Whatever the colour, nothing could detract from the fact that this was one beautiful woman.

Under any other circumstance he would be tempted to let a whistle escape his lips.

Her long, swanlike neck moved but she didn't speak. Those strange eyes did not leave his face.

He stopped a foot away from her and asked in English, 'Who are you?'

Her lips tightened and she hugged herself even harder, giving a quick shake of her head.

'Why are you here?'

But still she didn't speak. If he hadn't caught the obscenities she'd screeched when she'd exploded out of the bathroom, he could believe she was mute.

If she hadn't broken into his property, he would feel bad for her obvious fright.

'You know this is private property? *Sì?*' he tried again, speaking slowly. Dante's English was fluent but his accent thick. 'This cottage is empty but it belongs to me.'

The strange yet beautiful eyes suddenly narrowed and in that slight movement he realised fear wasn't the primary emotion being thrown at him, it was loathing.

'My backside does it belong to you.' She straightened. Her strong accent registered in his brain as Irish. 'This cottage is part of your father's estate and should be shared with your sister.'

Anger swelled in him.

So that was what this was all about? Another charlatan pretending to be Salvatore Moncada's secret love-child in the hope of grabbing a portion of Dante's inheritance. What did this make? Eight or nine fraudsters since his father's death three months ago? Or was this someone Dante's lawyer had already sent packing but thought they would chance their luck one more time and try and convince Salvatore's legitimate child herself?

As a means of getting his attention this woman had played a master stroke.

What a shame for her that it would end in her arrest and deportation.

'If I had a secret sister I'm sure I would be open to sharing a portion of my father's estate with her, but—'

'There's no *if* about it,' she interrupted. 'You *do* have a sister and I have the proof with me.'

Something in her tone cut the retort from his tongue.

Dante stared even harder at the beautiful face before him as his veins slowly turned to ice.

Did this truculently sexy woman really believe she was his…*sister*?

So *this* was Dante?

Aislin had seen many pictures of the cruel Sicilian intent on denying her sister what was morally hers but nothing could have prepared her for the sculptured reality stood before her.

In the flesh he was much taller than she'd expected, his hair thicker and darker. He had a lean, wiry muscularity she hadn't expected either. Nor had the pictures done justice to the rest of him. His thick, dark beard couldn't hide the chiselled jawline or downplay the firm, sensuous lips resting below a straight nose that could have been carved by a professional sculptor. Thick black brows rested above green eyes that could only be described as beautiful, and those eyes were staring at her with a combination of disgust and disbelief.

It hadn't escaped her attention that Dante was a good-looking man but she had not been prepared in the slightest for the raw sexiness that oozed from him.

His black shirt was unbuttoned at the neck and, while she kept her gaze fixed on his eyes, she'd glimpsed the dark hair poking through at the base of his throat.

Dante Moncada was the sexiest, most handsome man she had ever set eyes on and it thrilled with the same intensity that it repelled.

Despite the warmth she'd managed to inject into the walls from the log fire, a shiver ran up her spine, and she drew her towelling robe more tightly around her, wishing she could glue it to her body. It fell to her ankles but, with that green stare on her, she might as well have forgone it. She felt naked.

Beneath it she *was* naked.

It had been two days since she'd broken into this cottage. Two days she'd been living here, waiting for her presence to be noted and for the certain confrontation with this man to take place. But, seriously, did it have to occur the minute she stepped out of the shower?

So much for the cool, calm, no-nonsense first impression she'd hoped to make. In her head she'd created a scene where he stormed into the cottage and found her sitting serenely at the table studying, preferably wearing her reading glasses. Whenever Aislin wore those glasses, men tended to speak to her as if she had more than a single brain cell floating in her head.

Hearing the creak of the floorboards as Dante and his two goons had climbed the stairs had terrified her. She'd been instantly aware of the vulnerability of her position, thrown her still-wet body into the robe and wrenched the showerhead off as her only means of defence.

Dante must think he was dealing with a wailing banshee, an impression it was essential she correct immediately.

He took a step back, his left brow rising up and down. 'You believe you are my sister?'

She jutted her chin out to hide her discomfort at her nakedness beneath the robe. 'If you will be good enough to let me get dressed, I will explain everything. The kitchen is stocked with coffee.'

He gave a grunt of surprised laughter. 'You break into my home and want me to make you a drink?'

'I'm asking you to give me some privacy so I can make myself decent before we start arguing about the inheritance you are trying to keep for your greedy self. I'm simply pointing out that there is coffee if you wish to have one while you wait, and that I take mine with milk and one sugar.'

The green eyes flickered over her, taking in every inch of her body, before he blinked, gave the slightest of shudders and took another step back.

'I will leave you to dress,' he said curtly.

He closed the door behind him.

Aislin took a moment to force huge lungfuls of oxygen down her throat but Dante's departure seemed to have taken all the air with him. All that was left were the remnants of his cologne that even her non-perfumer self could tell with one sniff was expensive. Expensive and…sexy, just like the man it adhered to.

Knowing she needed to calm her thoughts or Dante would eat her alive, she pulled a pair of jeans, a silver jumper and underwear out of the wardrobe and hurried into the bathroom, locking the door behind her. She dressed quickly, ran her fingers through her damp hair then took one last fortifying breath before leaving the room to find Dante.

This confrontation was one she had prepared for. In theory, she had prepared for all eventualities, even if those eventualities had been cobbled together in a rush when they had learned Dante had sold the hundred acres in Florence and pocketed the proceeds into his already bulging bank account.

All she had to do was hold her nerve against this physically imposing man. His looks and scent did not count for jack. This man, a billionaire in his own right, had ridden roughshod over her sister's efforts to claim a share of their father's estate.

The stairs led into the cosy open-plan living area, where she found him sat on one of the sagging sofas, flicking through one of her university books. Two steaming mugs of coffee were laid on the table before him. His Goliath-proportioned sidekicks were nowhere to be seen.

His eyes narrowed at her approach and he waited in silence until she had sat herself in the farthest spot from him she could find.

He jabbed a finger onto the opened page of the textbook, the place where she had marked her name, as she had done since her school days. 'Tell me about yourself, Aislin O'Reilly.'

He pronounced her name 'Ass-lin', which under normal circumstances would have made her laugh.

She shook her head. For some reason her tongue struggled to work around this man.

He slammed the book on the table, making her jump. 'You claim to be my sister, so tell me about yourself. Show me your proof.'

She crossed her legs and met the intense green stare head-on. 'I'm not your sister. My sister, Orla, is your sister. I'm here as her representative.'

His brow furrowed. She could see him trying to work out what that made them in relation to each other.

'Orla and I have the same mother,' she supplied. 'You and Orla have the same father.'

Dante's lungs loosened at the confirmation that this intruder was not of his blood. The mere sway of her hips as she'd walked down the stairs had sent his senses springing to life. Dante was not particularly fussy when it came to women. He liked them in all shapes and sizes but to think he could find someone who was possibly his own sister desirable would have been enough to drive him straight to the nearest therapist.

'Where is the proof of this, Aislin?'

The lighting in the cottage against the darkly painted walls left much to be desired but now she sat close enough for him to see that the colour of the eyes ringing their loathing at him was grey. The black outer rim of the eyeballs contrasted starkly, making the grey appear translucent. Along with the angled tilt of her eyes, it gave the most extraordinary effect.

'It's Aislin,' she corrected, pronouncing it 'Ashling'.

'Ashling.' He practised it aloud. 'Aislin… An unusual name.'

The striking eyes held his without blinking. 'Not in Ireland it isn't.'

He shrugged. As unusual and interesting as her name was, there were far more important things to discuss. 'You say you have proof that… Orla? Is that her name?'

She nodded.

'That Orla is my sister. Let me see that proof.'

She got to her feet and walked to the small kitchen area, the curve of her bottom in her tight jeans a momentary distraction. From a small bag on the counter she took out an envelope and opened it on her walk back to him.

Pulling a sheet of paper out of the envelope, she handed it to him with a curt, 'Orla's birth certificate.'

Dante took the sheet from her with blood roaring in his ears. Slowly, he unfolded it.

He blinked a number of times to clear the filmy fog that had developed in his eyes.

The birth certificate was dated twenty-seven years ago. On the box labelled 'father' were the words *Salvatore Moncada.*

He rubbed his temples.

This didn't prove anything. This could be a forgery. Or, more likely, Aislin and Orla's mother—he scanned the certificate again and found Sinead O'Reilly named as the mother—had lied.

From the envelope still in her hand, Aislin plucked out a photograph and held it out to him.

He didn't want to look at it.

He *had* to look at it.

The photo was a headshot of two people, a young woman and a toddler boy.

A violent swell clenched and retracted in his stomach.

Both subjects in the photo had thick, dark-brown hair, the exact shade of Dante's.

The woman had green eyes the exact shade of Dante's.

## CHAPTER TWO

AISLIN TOOK IN the ashen hue Dante's olive skin had turned and experienced a stab of sympathy to witness the penny drop in that arrogant head.

She placed the envelope on the table and grabbed the coffee he'd made for her, unable to understand why her hands shook. It felt as if her entire insides were shaking, tiny vibrations quivering through her bones and veins.

She told herself it was because of the situation, her body preparing itself for the biggest fight it had ever undertaken. It was nothing to do with Dante himself.

The value of this cottage and its land were peanuts for a man of Dante's wealth but for her sister it meant the world. It would enable her to buy a home that Finn could live in with the freedom to be as normal a child as his condition allowed. That was all Orla wanted—a decent home in which to raise her son.

Aislin loved her nephew with her whole heart. Finn *was* her heart. For months she'd sat by his side as he'd lain in that awful incubator in the neonatal intensive care nursery, willing his tiny body to grow, for his lungs to work on their own; praying that one day he would be strong enough to go home…to survive.

The little fighter had survived, but not without complications. His entire life would be a fight and Aislin was prepared to do whatever necessary to make that fight more bearable.

Dante's lawyer had blocked her sister's every attempt for recognition. Aislin had flown to Sicily determined to confront Dante in person but, again, had been blocked. The security around him was too tight for her to get a foot through it. Breaking into this cottage had been the last desperate resort.

After a length of time had passed that seemed to be stretched by elastic, Dante finally looked up from the photo.

Her heart made the strangest clenching motion when his green eyes locked onto hers. There was a hardness in his stare.

'I have never heard of this woman. My father had many lovers. Many men and women have come forward since his death claiming to be his secret love-child. You give me a photograph and claim it is my sister…'

His thick Sicilian accent soaked into her skin as if her pores were breathing it in.

'I am claiming nothing—she *is* your sister. You can see the resemblance.'

He gave a tutting sound that was pure Sicilian. 'A convenient resemblance.'

'There is nothing convenient about it!' she retorted hotly, and would have added more had he not raised a palm up.

'If she is my sister, why did she wait until after my father's death to reveal herself?'

'She didn't need to reveal herself. Your father paid maintenance for her upbringing until she was eighteen.'

He sagged slightly at this revelation but it was the briefest of movements, his composure regained in a breath. 'That is something I can discover the truth of for myself.'

'It *is* the truth and, if you hadn't stonewalled her every attempt to speak to you, you would have all the facts at your fingertips.'

'My father acknowledged one child. Me. There was no talk of a secret sister, no death-bed confession.'

'That's not Orla's fault.'

'Would she still claim to be my sister if I were to tell you there is nothing left of his estate?'

'That's because you've sold it all off!'

The look he cast her was full of fake pity. 'My father was a gambling addict. He sold everything he could to fund his debts.'

'I've seen the list of assets.' That was the only thing Orla's useless lawyer had been able to get from Dante's terrifyingly efficient one. 'He was worth millions. Orla isn't being greedy. All she wants is a small share of it. Morally, she's entitled to that, even if you and your lawyer don't agree. I'm prepared to stage a sit-in in this cottage until you either sign it over to her or pay her off.'

Before Dante could laugh at Aislin's nerve, a lock of hair fell onto his forehead and over his eyes. He brushed it back. He needed to get it cut, another thing to add to his ever-long list of things to do.

'The law is on my side. Do you really believe that moving into this cottage—illegally—will get you anywhere?'

Her eyes spat fury at him. 'Possession is nine-tenths of the law.'

'Maybe in Ireland. But this is Sicily. My country. My property. My land. I can snap my fingers and have you removed from this cottage and expelled from the country.'

'Try it.' She jumped back to her feet and snatched the envelope off the table to pull yet another sheet of paper out of it. 'Try it and I will make sure every media outlet knows what you've done. This is not your land, it's part of your father's estate. All Orla wants is what she's entitled to, and this is the authority for me to handle things on her behalf.'

Dante ignored the letter, although he took note of the pretty hand holding it and the buffed, shapely nails. Then he slowly let his gaze drift upwards, over the curvy hips, the slender waist and the large breasts caressed lovingly in a soft, silver sweater. Simple clothing draped over an outstanding body. As her fragrance snaked its way back into his senses, he experienced a thickening in his loins. Disconcerted with this involuntary reaction to this woman, and at this moment in time, he reached for his coffee.

Dante freely admitted his libido was strong but the last time he'd experienced an inappropriate erection like this had been in a maths lesson almost two decades ago when his teacher had leaned over his desk to help him and her top had gaped open, exposing her cleavage.

He made a point of taking a large sip of the coffee, dragging his focus to the matter at hand. For instant coffee, it wasn't too bad, its heat a welcome respite from the cold that had settled in his spine.

The resemblance between himself and the woman in the photograph was astounding.

'Has your sister ever lived in Sicily?'

The neat, pretty eyebrows drew together. 'No.'

'Say for argument's sake that your assessment is correct and that my father really was worth millions when he died, what makes you think Orla would be entitled to anything? My father named me as his sole heir. She was not recognised as his child. You have to appreciate that my lawyer and I have been through this many times already.'

When the first fraudster had tried their hand at claiming on the estate, Dante and his lawyer had discussed all the legalities on the off-chance the fraudster was telling the truth.

'It might have been different if she had lived in my country at any point in her life. I suggest she pays a visit to a Sicilian lawyer and hears for herself that she has no rights.' He laughed, although humour was the last thing he felt right then. 'There is nothing for her to have. That list you have is old and dates from my grandfather's death. My father sold most of the assets on it. The family home never belonged to him and nor did the land in Florence—my grandparents put them in a trust for me to stop my father selling them to feed his gambling addiction.'

That hadn't stopped one of the fraudsters taking out an injunction to prevent Dante selling those assets, an injunction his lawyer had overturned in ten days. That fraudster was currently rotting in a Sicilian prison, awaiting trial for fraud.

'This cottage is all he had left and it is not for sale.' As dilapidated as the cottage was, Dante would never sell it. He wasn't a man for sentimentality but this was the one place where his childhood memories were only positive. His mother had loathed the cottage and thus it remained untainted by her long-ago desertion.

'Then pay Orla off. Even if what you say is true, and your grandparents bypassed your father, surely she's entitled to something? She knows she can't expect things to be fifty-fifty between you but morally she's entitled to something. She'll be happy to settle for the value of this cottage.'

He shook his head in a display of sympathy. Her approach was pitch-perfect, reason matched with a seeming lack of greed. The perfect cover for an outrageous act of fraud.

Dante had almost convinced himself she spoke the truth but that was impossible. His father would never have kept such a secret from him.

He was quite sure his lawyer, one of the most feared legal brains across the Mediterranean, would have been taken in too. Aislin clearly had the brains to match her beauty. She was an incredible actress.

'This cottage is worth no more than a hundred thousand euros,' he said, ensuring his voice contained just the right amount of commiseration. 'The land is worth about the same.'

'That might not be a lot of money to you but to Orla it's a fortune.'

'If it's worth so much to her then why is she not here? Why has she sent you to deal with it?'

'Because right now she doesn't want to leave Ireland. I'm portable—'

'Did she not want to face me?' The anger that had been simmering deep inside bubbled to the surface. 'Or did my *sister* think sending a beautiful woman in her place would blind me? Is that why you're here? To tempt me into giving this cottage to her?'

Her eyes widened, dark spots of angry colour forming again over the high cheekbones. 'Your mind belongs in a sewer.'

'I'm sure it does.' He rose slowly to his feet. 'You were showering when I came to the cottage. Was that deliberate? Were you keeping watch for me? Did my men being with me force you to change your plans? Did you realise then that you had taken on more than you could handle?'

He gave her no time to defend herself.

Stepping to where she had backed herself against the kitchen unit, he continued, 'Admit it, this is all a bag of lies. What do they call it in English, when a person steals another's image and passes it off as their own?'

The colour spread from her cheekbones to suffuse her entire face, the plump lips clamping tightly together as he stared down at her, daring her to tell the truth.

A sudden image came into his head of those plump lips parting for him…

Heat coiled through his loins again and he breathed deeply to drive it away, only to inhale another lungful of her beautiful scent.

Dante gritted his teeth and waved the photograph still in his hand at her. 'How long did you search for the perfect image that you could use to pretend to be my long-lost sister?'

In one sharp but graceful movement, she snatched it from his hand and stabbed a finger at the toddler's face.

'Did you not even look at the boy Orla's holding?' she snarled. 'That's your nephew.'

'Of course it is. What better than a beautiful child to pull on a man's heartstrings and charm him into giving you money? I have to say, of all the hustlers who have tried to con me, you, *dolcezza*, are by far the best.'

Her foot moved. For a moment Dante thought she was going to kick him.

Instead she spun around, grabbed her handbag and pulled her phone out.

In seconds she had it unlocked and was thrusting it in his face.

'What am I supposed to be looking at?' he asked drolly.

For someone who had to be a foot shorter than him, she raised herself magnificently. 'The photos. There must be a hundred of Finn on it and a load of Orla too.'

The coldness in his veins made a sharp return.

'Take the phone, damn you, and look!' She grabbed hold of his hand and pressed the phone into it.

A jolt ran through him at the touch of her skin on his, a charge that flowed through them both and had their eyes locking together in mutual shock.

After a pause that went on a beat too long, she moved her hand and stepped to the side, away from him.

Aislin dropped her eyes to the floor and rubbed her hands together, trying to negate the charge flowing through her veins.

Her heart beat so hard its thrum echoed in her ears.

She had not expected that. It had been like those times when she touched something and received a surprise charge of static. But those charges had always been unpleasant, something only a masochist would enjoy. The charge she had felt when touching Dante had been…

Not unpleasant at all.

'Please, look at it,' she whispered, summoning the courage to look back at him.

Aislin was not the greatest photographer in the world, and generally managed to chop the top off heads or get a partial thumb over the lens or get a blurry finish. But, however terrible the pictures were in comparison to the one she'd printed off for him, they were documentary proof that she wasn't lying; that she hadn't catfished Orla's identity; that her sister was Dante's half-sister.

Biologically, Orla was Aislin's half-sister too, but she had never thought of her as anything other than her whole sister. They'd been raised together, shared a room until Orla had left for university and been true sisters in every sense of the word. They'd protected each other, fought each other, played, loved and hated. No one could wind Aislin up better than Orla could and she knew it was the same for her sister.

Dante's Adam's apple moved a number of times before he slowly walked to the dining table and sat on the nearest chair, his focus solely on the photos of the two people she loved most in the world.

Her legs suddenly feeling weak too, she took the seat opposite him, close enough that she could hear him breathe, the deep breaths of someone whose life was in the process of being turned upside down.

Aislin knew that feeling. Orla's accident, which had resulted in Finn's premature birth, had turned their world upside down. Life as they knew it had come to a stop that day, three years ago.

She could not help but feel for Dante, trying to imagine what it would feel like to discover a family secret of this magnitude.

It must be shattering.

Her own dad had fathered two more children after his split with her mum but there had been no deception about it, just an awareness that he'd created a new family unit that Aislin was a part of, if somewhat removed from. Her mother, for all her many faults, was no liar. Sometimes Aislin had wished her mum *was* a liar. It would have saved a lot of angst and heartbreak.

'I'm not a hustler,' she said softly after a good two minutes that felt more like two hours had passed, the only sound Dante's breaths and the swipe of his thumb against the screen of her phone. 'Orla is as much your sister as she is mine and Finn is as much your nephew too. I know she'll be happy to take a DNA test if you think it necessary.'

More silence fell until he came to a photo that made him peer more closely. Then he turned the phone to her. 'Why is he in hospital? What are those things on his head?'

She looked at her darling nephew, smiling in his hospital bed. 'That was taken six months ago when he went for an EEG.'

'What's that?'

'It measures brainwaves. He was born prematurely and has cerebral palsy. One of the side effects of that, which he has since been diagnosed with, is severe epilepsy. It's the reason Orla didn't come to Sicily herself—she's terrified to leave him. Finn's condition is the reason she wants a share of the inheritance. She honestly is not being greedy. She just wants a home he can be safe in.' She was silent for a moment before adding, 'That's all I want for him too. I'm sorry for breaking into your cottage. Honestly, I'm not normally one for criminal behaviour, but we're desperate. Please, Dante, Finn is your nephew. We need your help.'

Dante expelled a long breath and put the phone on the table, then dropped his pounding head and kneaded his fingers into the back of his skull.

He felt sick.

If the evidence was to be believed—and, no matter how hard he strove to find a new angle to disprove it, the evidence appeared compelling—he had a sister and a nephew. A sick nephew.

Another wave of nausea ripped through him.

His father had lied to him.

He thought back to Orla's date of birth. He would have been seven when she'd been born. His mother had divorced his father when he was seven.

Did his mother know he had a sister? Had she conspired to keep it secret too?

So many thoughts crowded in his head but stronger than all of them was the image of the tiny boy, his nephew, lying on that hospital bed, hooked to a machine via a dozen tubes stuck to his head.

'How old is he?'

'A month shy of three.'

He didn't want to hear the sympathy now ringing from the soft Irish brogue. He could feel it too, radiating from her.

This woman felt sorry for *him*?

She didn't know him. All they shared was a sister. And a sick nephew.

He muttered a curse.

He raised his head and looked Aislin square in the eye.

Yes, there was compassion in the reflected stare, but also a healthy wariness.

He steepled his fingers across the bridge of his nose and thought hard, pushing aside the emotions crowding him, sharpening his wits and clearing his mind.

He had a business deal to salvage with the D'Amores before he could begin to think about this, never mind deal with it. The clock was ticking. Five days to salvage the biggest deal of his life. Unless he could convince Riccardo that his own playboy days were behind him and prove his parents' faults were not his, then the deal for the exclusivity agreement would be lost for good. On Monday Riccardo intended to sign it with Dante's biggest rival.

One lesson he had learned at a young age was that nothing must come before business. His father had allowed emotions and addiction to take first place and had lost everything for it.

Yet still that image of the boy, his nephew, stayed lodged in the forefront of his mind, and as he stared into the grey eyes of this woman who had just told him his entire life had been a lie, the kernel of an idea flared.

He swept his eyes again over the curvy body and imagined it dressed in expensive couture, and the hair whose colour he still couldn't determine beautifully styled.

Aislin was a stranger in his country. No one knew

her. She was clearly intelligent. And she was beautiful enough that no one would think twice to see her on his arm.

Despite her beauty, she was far removed from the women he normally dated…

'I spoke the truth. My father died penniless,' he told her slowly. 'I gave him an allowance and paid his bills but, other than this cottage, he had nothing left to his name. Under Sicilian law, your sister is not even entitled to a share of that.'

Aislin closed her eyes and slumped in her chair.

The tone of his words held the ring of truth.

Defeat loomed so large she lost the strength to correct him, to say loud and proud that Orla was his sister too.

Aislin was a penniless student. Orla was a penniless single mother still fighting the insurance company for compensation for the damage to her son. They'd pooled the spare cash they'd had between them to instruct that rubbish lawyer who hadn't even bothered to read up properly on Sicilian inheritance laws. Her open-ended return flight here and the car hire had left them skint.

If there was a loophole they could exploit to get something, they had no money left with which to do it.

'This cottage and the land it stands on have been in my family for generations and I have no wish to sell,' he continued, breaking through her defeated thoughts. 'But I am prepared to give Orla half the value. Fifty-fifty.'

She snapped her eyes back open and met his unblinking gaze. 'Really?'

He nodded. 'One hundred thousand euros. It will

be conditional on her taking a DNA test, but we can get that arranged soon. If the test comes back as positive, the money is hers.'

The relief that surged through her at that moment was enough to punch all the breath out of her.

She covered her mouth with a trembling hand. 'Thank you. You don't know what that means—'

'I also have an offer for you,' he cut in before she could get carried away with her thanks. 'An offer that is not DNA-conditional.'

'What kind of offer?'

'A mutually beneficial one.' His eyes narrowed and he rocked his head as if he were thinking. Then he gave one final nod and stilled. 'I have a wedding to attend this weekend. I want you to come with me.'

'You want me to come to a wedding with you?'

'*Sì*. And in return I will pay you one million euros.'

## CHAPTER THREE

'BUT...' AISLIN COULDN'T form anything more than that one syllable. Dante's offer had thrown her completely.

His smile was rueful. 'My offer is simple, *dolcezza*. You come to the wedding with me and I give you a million euros.'

He pronounced it *'seemple'*, a quirk she would have found endearing if her brain hadn't frozen into a stunned snowball.

'You want to pay me to come to a wedding with you?'

*'Sì.'* He unfolded his arms and spread his hands. 'The money will be yours. You can give as much or as little of it to your sister.'

'Won't your girlfriend mind?'

As soon as the words left her mouth, Aislin wanted to kick herself.

His beautifully thick brown eyebrows rose in perfect timing with the flame of colour she could feel rising over her face. 'Did you research me?'

'I saw a picture of you together when I was thinking up ways to get your attention,' she muttered, dropping her eyes to examine her fingernails, desperately trying to affect nonchalance.

She hadn't been researching *him*, more trying to get

a handle on the man in the days before she'd set off for Sicily, trying to decide the best way to cut through the minders and hangers-on to grab his attention for long enough to have the conversation they were now having… A conversation that had taken a most bizarre turn that she was struggling to get her head around.

What she had learned was that Dante Moncada was a man any right-thinking woman would steer a million miles away from. His father had been a Lothario who had seduced Aislin's mother when she'd still been a teenager, and all the evidence pointed to Dante being of the same 'love them and leave them' mould. Dante did not need to pay someone to attend a wedding with him. She would hazard a guess that, if he asked a roomful of women if any wanted to go with him, ninety-nine per cent of them would bob their heads up to agree like over-caffeinated meerkats.

Aislin was part of the one per cent who would duck under a table rather than accept. She'd been there, done that, stupidly having fallen for the biggest playboy on campus, believing his declarations of love and respect; believing they'd had a future that involved marriage and babies, only to find him in bed with one of her housemates mere weeks after her sister's accident.

If she was ever stupid enough to get involved with a man again, her preference would be for a boring, gaming-obsessed hermit with zero libido who had an abhorrence of the outside world and would thus never be in a position or have the mind-space to cheat.

Not a man like Dante. Not this man, who was sexier and more handsome than should be legal.

She could practically smell the testosterone and

pheromones wafting from him. They soaked into her pores in the same way his amazing deep voice did, sensitising her skin and settling deep inside her in a way that was, quite frankly, terrifying.

But a million euros…?

'I ended it with Lola a month ago.' He leaned forward, a sudden, unexpected gleam appearing in his eyes.

Her heart thumped, the beat ricocheting through her like a tsunami.

It took a huge amount of effort to keep her voice steady. 'But you must have a heap of women you could take and not have to pay them for it.'

'None of them are suitable.'

'What does that mean?'

'I need to make an impression on someone and having you on my arm will assist in that.'

'A million dollars for one afternoon…?'

'I never said it would be for an afternoon. The celebrations will take place over the coming weekend.'

She tugged at her ponytail. 'Weekend?'

'Aislin, the groom is one of Sicily's richest men. It is a necessity that his wedding be the biggest and flashiest it can be.'

She almost laughed at the deadpan way he explained it.

She didn't need to ask who the richest man in Sicily was.

'If I'm going to accept your offer, what else do I need to know?'

'Nothing… Apart from that I will be introducing you as my fiancée.'

*'What?'* Aislin winced at the squeakiness of her tone.

'I require you to play the role of my fiancée.' His

grin was wide with just a touch of ruefulness. The deadened, shocked look that had rung from his eyes only a few minutes before had gone. Now they sparkled with life and the effect was almost hypnotising.

She blinked the effect away.

'Why do you need a fiancée?'

'Because the father of the bride thinks going into business with me will damage his reputation.'

'How?'

'I will go through the reasons once I have your agreement on the matter. I appreciate it is a lot to take in so I'm going to leave you to sleep on it. You can give me your answer in the morning. If you're in agreement then I shall take you home with me and give you more details. We will have a few days to get to know each other and work on putting on a convincing act.'

'And if I say no?'

He shrugged. 'If you say no, then no million euros.'

'What about the hundred thousand you said you would give Orla?'

'That is a separate matter and dependent on the DNA test. Your decision will not affect that.'

'Do you promise?' She knew it was a childish way of asking but she didn't care. A hundred thousand euros was too great a sum to play games with.

But a million euros… That was a figure she could scarcely comprehend. That was life-changing.

His handsome features fell into seriousness. He inclined his head before rising to his feet. 'Whatever you decide, and whatever the outcome, that money for Orla will remain separate from it. You have my word.'

She didn't have the faintest idea why but she believed him.

* * *

Dante greeted the housekeeper, who made an almost convincing job of not acting surprised to see him and at such a late hour, and strolled through his old family home as he had done a thousand times before.

This was the sprawling seafront villa he'd grown up in, just as his father had. A decade ago, to prevent the villa being used as collateral against his son's gambling debts, his grandfather had signed it over to Dante.

Although the villa had been technically his for all these years, as far as he'd been concerned it had remained his father's to do with as he pleased…apart from sell it.

With his father dead, he still didn't know what to do with it. Unspoken had been his grandfather's wish that one day Dante would settle down, marry, start a family and raise them in this home.

Dante liked city life. He liked being single. What good was marriage for? All he had ever seen of it was bitterness, greed and spite. His grandparents had been married for forty-eight years until his grandmother's death. If they were a template for the longevity of marriage, they could forget it. His grandfather had spent the three years from her death until his own celebrating being rid of her. Dante had been quite sure his grandfather's shaking shoulders at her funeral had been through laughter rather than tears.

At the far end of the villa was his father's study. In the days after his death, Dante had holed himself in there, finding comfort in the room that had been quintessentially his father.

He pushed the door open and inhaled the familiar, if now fading, scent of bourbon and cigars.

This was the room Dante had sneaked into as a small boy, the desk he would hide under until his father appeared and he would jump out at him, and his father would pretend to shout in fright every single time.

He sat on the chair his father had called his own, the chair on which his father had sat Dante on his lap, held him tightly and told him his mother had left and that it would be just the two of them from now on.

This was the room his father had given Dante his first drink of bourbon in, the room in which he'd relayed the deaths of family members, the room where he'd confessed his dire financial situation and begged his only son for a loan to pay off his gambling debts. The latter had taken place so many times Dante had lost count.

A lifetime of memories, good and bad, flooded him and it took a few minutes for him to gather himself together and for the fresh wave of grief to pass.

He opened his father's laptop. When he'd opened it the first time after his father's death he'd guessed the password correctly—Dante's name and date of birth. That had been a bittersweet moment.

Keying the password in this time, all he tasted was bitterness.

Had his father really kept a sister secret from him for all these years?

Aislin claimed his father had paid maintenance for Orla. If there was evidence of it, it would be on here somewhere.

He had a sister. His gut told him that and he did not doubt the DNA test would prove a match.

But had his father known or had Sinead O'Reilly kept Orla's existence a secret from him and lied to her daughters about maintenance being paid?

Dante sent a silent prayer that Sinead was a liar and logged onto his father's saved bank statements.

Damn it, they only went back eight years.

He drummed his fingers on the desk. Where would the paper statements be from the years before that? His father had been a terrible hoarder so they would be here somewhere…

The filing cabinet, of course.

An hour later and he was sat on the carpeted floor, paperwork strewn around him. In his hand was the evidence he'd been seeking but praying he wouldn't find.

Until nine years ago, coincidentally the year Orla had turned eighteen, his father had paid the sum of two thousand euros every month to a bank account in Ireland.

Aislin hovered by the front window of the cottage, peering out intermittently while she waited for Dante.

Nerves in the form of butterflies rampaged in her belly.

Her bags were packed and waiting by the front door. She'd spent most of the night fighting the urge to flee to the airport.

A hundred thousand euros was a substantial amount of money but a million was life-changing. Orla could buy a home, modify it to cater to all Finn's needs and have change to spare at the end of it. She could take him on holiday. She could buy him a high-tech wheelchair. She could buy a car.

So Aislin had stayed in the cold cottage, hardly sleeping, her mind whirling like a dervish, trying to understand why her instinct was to run.

A million euros to attend a wedding! All her family's problems solved in one weekend!

Restless, she paced the living area.

She'd been prepared to break into the cottage and stage a sit-in in defiance of a powerful billionaire; had been prepared to stay there for as long as it took for him to develop a conscience.

She had not expected it to develop so quickly or easily.

His agreement to give Orla half the value of the cottage and its land had proven his conscience. That he was insisting on a DNA test was not surprising and not something she could blame him for. Dante was no fool. No one who reached the heights in business he had got there by taking people at face value.

She had expected an arrogant monster and found, instead, an arrogant man who could be compelled to listen to reason.

So why was she so resistant to spending a few days with him when the reward for doing so was so great?

A loud rap on the front door made her jump and, when Dante strode through the front door, her heart jumped too, right into her throat.

She'd opened the shutters earlier and spring sunlight poured into the cottage. Dante seemed to glow with it.

Dressed in a navy shirt, snug black jeans and an obviously expensive straight leather jacket, his handsome features were more pronounced than they'd been the evening before, the texture of his dark hair thicker and smoother, the green eyes that found hers brighter.

But there was something unkempt about his appearance too. He looked like a man who had spent the night at the bottom of a bottle of rum rather than in a bed. The effect only made him sexier. A pulse set off deep inside her, warmth gathering low in the most intimate of places…

Her reason for resistance suddenly became obvious.

This wasn't mere appreciation of a handsome, sexy man. She was attracted to him.

Aislin was attracted to Dante Moncada. Properly, heart-beatingly, swoon-makingly attracted.

'You are still here,' he stated as he closed the door.

'Well spotted, Einstein.'

Okay, so she was attracted to him. That was nothing to panic about. It didn't mean her brain cells had to become goo around him. She had overcome much worse than an unwelcome attraction to a gorgeous man before. If there was one thing Aislin had it was an abundance of self-control. How else could she have sat through all those awful meetings with the patronising social workers and other officials who'd all seemed determined to deny her the right to be Finn's legal guardian, while Orla had recovered from her horrific injuries, and not have punched any of them?

The slightest spark emerged in the green of his bloodshot eyes. 'Einstein would have killed for my IQ.'

Her lips twitched to break into a smile. 'And your modesty, I'm sure.'

He grinned. 'Am I to assume you're going to accept my offer?'

'A million euros to act as your arm candy for a few days? Yep, I can do that.' She could deal with attraction. Deal with it by ignoring it and keeping her wits sharp. 'But, before I accept your deal, I should point out that no one is going to believe we're engaged. You've only just dumped your last girlfriend.'

He winked, sank onto the sofa and stretched his legs out. His legs were so long his feet slid under the coffee table. 'Anyone who knows me knows I'm a fast mover.'

'That's nothing to be proud of,' she said tartly.

'Trust me, I know when to go slow.'

Heated colour spread like wildfire over her cheeks. 'I won't accept any funny business.'

She needed to make that very clear. Just because her body reacted so strongly to him did not mean she had any intention of allowing anything to happen between them. She would not be one of those over-caffeinated bobbing meerkats.

Dante could curse himself. He hadn't meant to make innuendoes but the opportunity had presented itself in irresistible fashion. 'You are speaking of sex?'

Her face now flamed so brightly it was quite possible it could explode.

'You have nothing to fear. This arrangement is strictly business. The bride and groom both come from religious families and will put us in separate rooms for the sake of appearances.'

After a terrible night when his brain had refused to shut down, even after he'd thrown the best part of a bottle of bourbon down his neck to assist it, he'd come to the conclusion that this deal *had* to be platonic. In any other circumstance he would go all-out to seduce Aislin but seduction would add too many complications. He needed to keep his head focused on salvaging the business deal, and that was before he added the small detail of Aislin being the sister of his father's secret love-child.

If he didn't believe she was the perfect woman to make Riccardo D'Amore believe him to be a changed man he would have called the whole thing off. But she *was* perfect. Not only was she not of their world but she had a working brain in her beautiful head and a firm commitment to family Riccardo would adore.

All Dante had to do was keep his hands off her, which he had a great feeling would be easier said than done.

Promises made in the twilight hours were much harder to keep in daylight when her scent coiled around his senses. In the daylight, Aislin was more than beautiful, her beauty enhanced now her hair was dry and its vibrant colour there for him to glory in, a deep russet that reminded him of fallen autumn leaves. It made him think of a fox, which he thought an apt word to describe her. She'd stolen into his cottage like a fox. An exquisite fox.

Today she'd dressed in black leggings, an oversized khaki jumper fraying on the left sleeve and scuffed black ankle boots. These were clothes designed for comfort, obviously old and worn, yet he found them as sexy as if she were wearing a tight cocktail dress with all her currently hidden cleavage on show.

She rubbed her hands over her arms, inadvertently pushing against those same breasts he'd just been imagining. 'As long as we're clear on things being platonic then that's grand.'

'Is there anything else you want to bring up? Because we need to get going.'

Those strange eyes were back on him again, penetrating like lasers. It was the strangest of feelings; unnerving yet weirdly erotic. 'I want half the money now.'

'No.'

'I need a guarantee. A form of surety. I don't want to spend a weekend pretending to like you only to have you then refuse to hand the money over.'

'You don't like me?'

'How do I know if I like you? I don't know you, certainly not well enough to trust you.'

Her lack of sycophancy was refreshing. She was direct, her mouth as unfiltered as her inherent sexiness. 'Ten thousand.'

'That's peanuts.'

'How much money do you have in your bank account?'

'The dust of a bag of peanuts.'

He bit back a laugh at her phrasing and spread his hands in a 'there you are' gesture.

She fixed him with a stare that made him think she would make an excellent teacher. It was a look that would shut a classroom full of screaming kids up.

He shook his head and gave an exaggerated sigh. '*Va bene*. I can be reasonable. Fifty thousand up front, in cash or transferred into a bank account of your choice, the remainder on Sunday evening. Deal?'

Her exquisitely beautiful face took on the expression of someone sucking an extra-sour lemon. Then she jerked her head into a nod. 'Yes. Deal.'

He rubbed his hands together and got to his feet. '*Eccellente*. Let's get going.'

'Transfer the money and then we can go.'

'You don't want it in cash?'

'I'd prefer it transferred.'

He sighed and pulled his phone out of his jacket pocket. 'Name of the account?'

'Miss Orla O'Reilly.'

He looked up briefly with a frown. 'You don't want it in your own account?'

'The money's not for me. It's for our sister and nephew. Orla's skint and the money you're going to give her once you've had the DNA test could take weeks to come through.'

'You're not going to keep any of the million for yourself?'

'I'll get her to buy me a pizza from it.'

Was she for real? 'Are you looking for a sainthood?'

She threw her schoolteacher stare at him again.

He shrugged. If she wanted to let the entire million slip through her fingers, that was her loss. 'The account details?'

She recited them to him.

He looked up from his phone again. 'You know your sister's bank details by heart?'

'She was in a bad car accident three years ago that left her in a coma. I took care of all her finances and stuff while she was in hospital and recovering from her injuries.'

'Is that why her son was born prematurely?'

A dimness filtered over the grey eyes. She nodded.

Why this information should make his finger hover over the sum he was about to transfer, he did not know.

This time yesterday he hadn't even known of Orla's existence.

Had his father known she'd been injured?

Had his father known he had a grandchild?

A fresh barb sliced through him at the reminder of the secrets and lies his father had kept from him for twenty-seven years.

Dante stared at the beautiful redhead, knowing he had to keep his focus on the primary reason for keeping her in Sicily and paying her such a substantial amount of money. Aislin was the key to convincing Riccardo D'Amore that he was not the sum of his parents' parts. Just because they shared a sister did not mean he could allow himself to be sidetracked. Orla's accident was history…

But the after-effects lived on in her son. His nephew.

They were nothing to do with him, he told himself grimly. They were strangers to him and would remain that way. A shared bloodline did not make them family and, even if it did, Dante had had enough of family.

He'd loved his mother with all his boyish heart and she'd abandoned him. He'd been close to his grandparents but their constant sniping and bad-mouthing of each other, and their respective expectations that he would take sides, had been a drain. His extended family were just as bad. He'd adored his father. Salvatore had been a fantastic if unconventional father when Dante had been small, father and son always there for each other through all the ups and downs life had thrown at them; and now he'd learned that beneath that closeness had been the most monstrous of secrets.

His father had been a gambler and a playboy but Dante would have trusted him with his life.

Turned out his father had been the greatest liar of them all.

Why embrace a sister when every other member of his bloodline had lied, abandoned or emotionally abused him?

No more. He was better on his own.

He hit the confirmation button then went through the additional security needed to transfer such a large sum. Anti-money-laundering regulations were the bane of the honest businessman's life. 'Done.'

He held the phone for her to see. 'The money will credit your sister's account by the end of the working day.'

She peered at it with a furrowed brow. 'You transferred two hundred thousand?'

He nodded tersely. 'I've upheld my end of the deal. Now we can go.'

# CHAPTER FOUR

AISLIN GAZED OUT of the car window. The drive from the cottage to Palermo had taken her from farmed fields and intense greenery to the bright lights of Sicily's capital in only twenty minutes.

Thankfully Dante had sat in the front next to his driver, enabling her to relax into the journey and not spend the trip fighting her growing awareness of him.

The gleam she'd seen in his eyes a few times had made her think he might be aware of her in the same way, but his declaration that this was purely a business agreement had put paid to that notion.

Her limited experience with men meant her instincts could not be relied on. Growing up in a small village in Kerry, there had been a shortage of boys to play with. Secondary school had not been much better on the boy front. By the time she'd started university she'd been desperate for a boyfriend but on her first day had overheard a group of boys ranking the girls on the size of their breasts, their 'spreadability' and their looks. It had been enough to make her vomit and, from that point on, she'd kept males at a distance, willing to be friends but not anything more. Some girls might have been happy to be marked out of ten on their prowess but she was not one of them.

It was in the summer term of her second year that Patrick had taken an interest her. Far from immediately trying to dive into her knickers, he'd made an effort to woo her. He'd brought her flowers. He'd asked for her help with an assignment—without a boyfriend to distract her, Aislin had soon distinguished herself as a swot—and it had filled her silly little head with pride that the most popular lad in her year was interested in *her*.

Weeks later, they'd started dating. Words of love and respect were exchanged, words she'd believed. Six months on, Orla had been driving in a heavy storm when an approaching car had lost control and smashed head-on into hers. Patrick, resenting Aislin's devotion to her comatose sister and prematurely born nephew, had wasted no time in hooking up with Aislin's housemate, a girl she had considered a good friend.

She hadn't dated anyone since. In all honesty, even if she'd wanted to, which she didn't, there hadn't been the space in her life to date.

Dante was the first man to occupy her thoughts in three years and, compared to his playboy antics, Patrick was a rank amateur.

She didn't know if it made it better or worse that Dante didn't fancy her. It shouldn't matter at all.

This deal was strictly business.

She couldn't work him out. One minute he was haggling over the upfront payment, driving down her demands, the next transferring four times the amount they had settled on.

So far, she hadn't dared tell Orla about the deal,

fearful of building her hopes up. She didn't think Dante would be able to stop the payment but he was a powerful man. Beneath the affable exterior lay a darkness. She had no idea what he was capable of.

It had been dark when she'd landed four days ago, too dark for her to appreciate Palermo's astounding beauty, especially as she'd been trying to navigate unfamiliar streets in a rental car and driving on a different side of the road than she was used to.

She'd almost forgotten about that rental car. Thankfully, Dante had given the keys to one of his goons with instructions to take it back to the airport.

Driving in daylight through Palermo was like stepping into the medieval past. Were it not for the busy narrow streets filled with people in modern dress, she could believe she'd slipped into a time vortex.

Expecting to be taken to a secluded palatial home guarded with Rottweilers and more goons of the armed variety, she was momentarily taken aback when Dante's driver pulled up in a street that was only a little wider than the luxurious vehicle they were in, stopping beside a long terrace of five-storey apartments. The street was clean and pretty, the exterior walls painted cream, iron balconies beneath all the upper windows with hanging baskets of flowers creating colour, a few scooters parked close to the walls.

Dante craned his neck to talk to her. 'We are here.'

'This is your home?'

She pressed her face against the window for a better look, certain he was having a laugh at her expense. This was an ordinary residential street. Dante was a billionaire. Shouldn't his main home—during the course of her research she'd discovered he owned a heap of opulent city apartments across Europe—be flashier?

A young, skinny lad in a leather jacket that must have cost a fraction of the price Dante had paid for his suddenly appeared from nowhere and opened Dante's door.

Dante unfolded his legs from the car, shook the boy's hand with his right hand whilst slapping his shoulder with his left and chatted animatedly with him while the driver opened Aislin's door and helped her out.

The boot of the car flipped open and the young lad broke away from the conversation to grab Aislin's suitcase and carry it to the arched door at the end of the row, a nondescript piece of wood she would have trouble distinguishing from the others.

Amusement danced in Dante's eyes as he indicated for Aislin to follow the boy inside.

She entered warily.

Was this all an elaborate hoax to punish her for breaking into his father's cottage? Was he leading her along, only pretending to believe her about Orla and Finn?

As with the exterior of the building, the interior was nothing to write home about. Plain concrete stairs led to the top floor and was mercifully free of graffiti or any pungent smells.

Instead of climbing the stairs, Dante punched the lift button. With a loud ping, the door opened.

Aislin blinked.

The lift was thickly carpeted. A whole side was a mirror without a single smear. It was the kind of elevator one would expect to see in a posh hotel.

She didn't feel any movement as they journeyed to the top floor. She followed Dante out into a small, square landing area with only one door. A grilled security partition had been drawn back from across it.

Before he could reach the door, the skinny teenager walked out of it.

Dante spoke briefly with Ciro, pressed some money in his hand then walked into the apartment as Ciro stepped into the lift.

He'd made it across the reception area before he realised Aislin had failed to follow him.

He turned to find her hovering with her back pressed to the wall beside the lift.

'Are you coming?'

'This isn't some kind of joke, is it?' she asked doubtfully.

'No joke. There is nothing to fear.'

Her grey eyes held his for an age before she blinked and made tentative steps to the threshold.

When she crossed it the whisper of a gasp flew from her mouth.

'Not what you were expecting?'

She shook her tilted head, eyes darting over the high-carved ceilings.

'Wait until you see the rest of it.' He pushed the double doors open and stepped inside.

Her gasp this time was audible.

'You like it?'

'I don't know...'

Dante always enjoyed watching people's reaction to his main home. He'd bought the first three adjacent apartments a decade ago then spent a year purchasing the other apartments until the whole street bar one ground-floor apartment was his. He hadn't had to use the strong-arm tactics many of his compatriots with his wealth and power would have used to convince the other owners to sell. Offering twice the listed value for each apartment had produced the same results and allowed him to sleep at night. He now employed the elderly couple who had refused to sell to be his eyes and ears. The remaining ground-floor apartments he used as homes for his staff. Knowing protection was on hand if he needed it without having his personal space encroached also allowed him to sleep well.

All the apartments on floors one to five had been knocked through to create a sprawling home that was unimaginable from the outside. This was the place Dante called home. His other apartments had been bought for convenience and as investments.

She walked to one of the windows and peered out. 'Where's your garden?'

Of all the questions and reactions that usually followed a new visitor stepping inside, this was a first.

'I don't have one.'

The look she cast him with was more than suspicious. 'No garden? Not even on your roof?'

'There's a terrace with a swimming pool on the roof.' He'd had it enclosed to retain his privacy. If he wanted to wander around naked on the roof, he could, and no one on the surrounding streets would be any the wiser.

'That's handy in the winter.'

'It's heated, but if the weather gets too bad I use the pool on the first floor.'

'You have two swimming pools but no garden?'

'I have no need or desire for a garden.'

'What if you have children?'

'I have no wish for children.' For Dante children went hand in hand with marriage and he had no intention of ever marrying.

'Is that what we tell people?'

'What do you mean?'

'You're going to tell people we're engaged. If the guests are anything like those who attend Irish weddings, the first thing we'll be asked is when we plan to have children.'

'If asked, keep the answer vague—we want to enjoy our time together and have children in the future. Now, let me show you to your room—hopefully you will find it more to your liking than the rest of the house.'

'I never said I didn't like it,' Aislin protested, sensing his back had gone up. 'I live in a dinky house with Orla and Finn. This is a little much for me to get my head around.'

The tiny two-bed house was the same one she had grown up in. The one decent thing their mother had done for them, before she had decided to reclaim her lost youth by backpacking her way around Asia, was to transfer the tenancy of the house to Aislin and Orla. That had been five years ago. When she planned to return to Ireland was anyone's guess. Her eldest daughter's head-on car crash that had resulted in horrific injuries to Orla and the premature birth of her first grandchild had not been lure enough to bring Sinead O'Reilly back to her family.

The space in Dante's home was mind-blowing. Sunlight poured through the abundant windows and danced over the obviously expensive dark furnishings, creating light where the dark woods and dark leathers would have made it feel gloomy. She estimated her entire house could fit in the living area alone.

Seeing the richness of Dante's life with her own eyes was very different from imagining it, was so much more, in the exact same way Dante was so much more vibrant and sexier in the flesh.

'How are we going to convince anyone that I belong in your world?' she asked, suddenly anxious.

His startling green eyes held hers for a moment before his lips lifted into a grin. 'But that is the reason you are so perfect for the role of my fiancée. You're different. I am not used to people telling me my home is anything but the work of a creative genius. You are not like my usual lovers and are not from my world. Riccardo is going to love you.'

'Who's Riccardo?'

'Riccardo D'Amore is the man we need to convince.'

'But what do we need to convince him of? You still haven't properly explained why you're paying me to be your fiancée.'

They'd passed through a room dedicated to modern art, paintings adorning the walls, quirky sculptures on plinths, and now stood on a mezzanine overlooking another vast living area.

'I have been working on an important business deal with Riccardo's son, Alessio. It's an exclusive software deal that will allow me to break into the American market. My father's death attracted much publicity. All the obituaries spoke in length about his love of women and addiction to gambling. The stories sowed doubt in Riccardo's mind about my character. He believes I am too much like my father to be trusted and that doing business with me will have a detrimental effect on the D'Amore reputation. He has put a stop to the business deal.'

Dante caught the flash of outrage in her eyes. 'Can he do that?'

He nodded grimly. 'He can and he has. Alessio runs the company but Riccardo is still the majority shareholder.'

'So how will us pretending to be engaged change anything?'

'Riccardo married young, has always been faithful to his wife and had lots of babies. He believes that family is sacrosanct, that gambling is the work of the devil—I understand his point there—and that sex is for marriage. My family is famous for pursuing pleasure—in my mother's case marrying and divorcing on a whim—gambling, sex without discretion...all the things he believes are sins. He believes in family and roots. You are nothing like my usual lovers. You study, you're intelligent, you have a strong loyalty and attachment to your family.'

The textbooks on medieval Europe she had brought with her, which he had flicked through while waiting for her to dress the night before, had been well-thumbed, pages turned over at the corners, notes in a lively penmanship made in the margins. The books had been heavy in his hands, the words dense on the pages.

She stared back, drawing her plump lips in before saying, 'But how are we going to explain *us*? Sure, you say people know you as a fast mover, but this is rocket fast.'

Her lips were the perfect shade of pink, bringing to mind fresh raspberries. What would they taste like…?

The flame of desire he'd smothered since leaving the cottage earlier reignited.

Dante fought the heated tendrils snaking through his bloodstream and willed his body to remain passive.

He was not an adolescent. He was an adult male who'd had so many lovers their names and faces were indistinguishable from each other.

'We will stick to the truth as much as we can. You came to Sicily to meet me on your sister's behalf. We can pad the timing.'

'Our sister,' she corrected obstinately.

'*Our* sister,' he agreed with a sigh. He'd known Aislin for less than a day but already he was fully aware she could argue for Ireland. She had passion in her soul and was refreshingly unafraid to show it. 'We were immediately attracted to each other.' That was not a lie. Not for him. Dante could not remember ever having felt such an immediate attraction to anyone. 'In fact, we would go so far as to say it was love at first sight. You were so different to everyone I've ever known that I was helpless not to fall in love with you. In you I knew I'd found the woman I wanted to settle down with and spend the rest of my life with.'

As he finished speaking, he realised his voice had dropped to a whisper and that his body was straining towards her. There was an itch in his fingers to reach out and touch her, to brush a thumb against her cheek…

Her face tilted back as she gazed right back at him, her neck elongating with such grace his mouth prickled to graze over the delicate skin.

'Because I'm so different?' Her voice dropped to a whisper that mimicked his.

*'Sì.'* Compellingly different in all the ways that mattered. A beautiful russet fox that made his senses dance to a rhythm he'd never felt before.

He wanted to taste those lips. He wanted to touch those high cheekbones.

'And we tell the truth about Orla?'

The reminder of his father's lies and deception acted like a bucket of iced water being thrown over his head.

Breathing heavily, he stepped back, cleared his throat and said gruffly, 'Lies only unravel into a mess. Where possible, we stick to the truth. The only real deception will be in our intention to marry. Now, I have some business to wrap up before I can give you my undivided attention.

'Your room is the last on the left.' He pointed to the end of the wide corridor. 'Get settled, explore, make yourself at home and in an hour or so we can have lunch.'

An hour would be ample time to shake off the heat flowing through his veins and get his concentration back to where it should be.

He would be spending all his time with Aislin over the next five days and could not afford to let this attraction take over his rationality.

Taking Aislin as his lover would be a complication too far, even if the heavy weight in his loins begged to differ.

*Dio*, he'd never reacted so strongly to a woman before. This was off all the scales.

He disappeared into his office.

Stunned at his abrupt departure, Aislin stared at

the door Dante had closed sharply behind him, her heart beating so hard it felt as if it could burst through her ribs.

For a moment she'd thought he was going to kiss her.

Worse, her lips had tingled with anticipation of that kiss. More than her lips had tingled. Her entire body thrummed with an electricity that heated her core and had her fighting the urge to kick the door open.

Furious with herself, Aislin bit hard into her bottom lip.

She must stop imagining things. Just because she found him so attractive did *not* mean the feeling was mutual. And nor should she want it to be mutual.

This was Dante Moncada, Mr Love Them and Leave Them, the son of the man who had seduced her nineteen-year-old mother.

She would *not* be a bobbing meerkat for him. She would get control of this damnable attraction if it took her the entire time they were together.

# CHAPTER FIVE

AISLIN'S TORTURED THOUGHTS were momentarily shoved aside when she opened the door to the room Dante had said was hers.

This was a guest room?

This must once have been an entire apartment. Inside it lay a four-poster king-sized bed, a walk-in wardrobe twice the size of her bedroom in Ireland, a huge flat-screen television and other electrical gizmos she didn't recognise. Fresh flowers had been placed on all four windowsills and the leather sofa was a caramel colour, rather than the chocolate of his living rooms, making it marginally less masculine than what she had seen of the rest of his home.

She took a look in the private bathroom and found a humongous shower *and* a roll-top bath.

Aislin stood at the huge, gold-framed mirror and stared critically at her reflection.

Fingering a lock of her hair, she grimaced at the ends badly in need of snipping. When had she last had it cut? It had to be coming up to a year. She was lucky she'd been blessed with eyebrows that didn't require upkeep otherwise she would likely resemble a werewolf.

When had she last worn make-up? Not since Orla's accident. Vanity, like everything else in her life, had been forgotten about. She'd restarted her degree last autumn but, not wanting to study away from home this time round, had opted to finish it through distance learning. This allowed her to stay with her sister and nephew and be there to help them with whatever they needed.

What she would do with that degree when she was done she no longer knew. The life plan she'd mapped out for herself all those years ago belonged to a different Aislin.

She wrinkled her nose.

Three years of neglecting her appearance showed. No wonder she did nothing for Dante.

Presumably, her lack of glamour and ordinary looks would give weight to her being *nothing like his usual lovers*, she thought moodily. It had been nothing but a roundabout way of saying that he found her plain and unsexy.

She didn't want him to find her sexy!

Dante was paying her a million euros to act as his fiancée. There was no point griping that it was being offered due to her ordinariness.

Pulling a face at her reflection, she set off to explore the rest of Dante's home.

And what a home it was.

Aislin felt like the glamorous host of some kind of 'amazing interiors' television show. But without the glamour.

She imagined herself talking to a camera and sweeping her arms majestically, pointing out that, where concrete stairs led to the top floor outside, inside the stairs were all white marble. The top three floors had been transformed into two levels with enormously high ceilings, containing a kitchen any chef would purr with delight in, two dining rooms, six bedrooms of equal proportions to her own—none of which she did more than peek into, scared in case one of them belonged to Dante—three living rooms, more dedicated art rooms and even a water feature in the centre with a river of water snaking from it. The floor below...

A swimming pool the Romans would have considered decadent, complete with a gym and spa facilities...

Her phone buzzed.

She pulled it out of her back pocket and answered her sister's call.

'Ash, I've just received an email from the bank notifying me of a credit. I've checked, two hundred thousand euros has been put in. *Two hundred thousand!* From Dante Moncada! What's going on? You said he was going to give me a hundred thousand when the DNA test's done.'

'It's actually credited?'

*'Yes!'* Orla burst into tears. Her sobs were so loud Aislin moved the phone from her ear until they quietened.

'Orla, breathe,' she instructed kindly.

The sobs were replaced by deep breaths. 'What's going on?'

'Well...' Aislin screwed her eyes shut as she said in a rush, 'Dante's paying me to pretend to be his fiancée for a weekend.'

'You what?' Tearful, overwhelmed Orla was suddenly replaced by bossy big sister Orla.

'It's for a business deal he's trying to salvage. He

needs to show a respectable face. Don't worry,' she hastened to add. 'There's nothing sinister or pervy about it.'

'If there's nothing pervy, why is he paying you all that money?'

'Actually…' She almost told her the grand total would be a million but stopped herself in time.

The full million was dependent on them fooling Riccardo D'Amore that they were a genuine couple. If Aislin didn't play her part well enough, she would forfeit the remainder.

'Actually what?' Orla prompted.

'Nothing. You have nothing to worry about. Dante finds me as attractive as a rhino. He needs a fake fiancée for one weekend to seal the business deal, he feels bad about your situation and wanted to do something to help.' She'd explained the night before about Salvatore dying with hardly a cent to his name and that under Sicilian law, which Aislin had checked up on herself with the help of the Internet, she would have a massive fight to get anything at all. 'By the way, you can't tell anyone.'

Her sister snorted. 'Who am I going to tell? Finn? The receptionist from the surgery?'

'Very funny. How is Finn today?'

'He's having a good day but he misses you. When will you be home?'

Aislin's heart clenched. She and Finn had a bond that was as strong as if she'd given birth to him herself. This was the first time they'd been parted since he'd been released into her care from the neonatal unit. 'All being well, early next week.'

'You will take care of yourself, won't you? Dante's reputation with women is awful.'

'I'm not his type, so stop worrying.'

'Has he said anything about wanting to meet me?'

'Not yet.' Not a single word. 'I think he wants to get this business deal done with first. It's very important to him.'

'More important than me and Finn?'

'He just needs time to process the fact he has a sister,' she reminded her gently, smothering her instinct to tell Orla it would be better if Dante remained only a name in her life. The last thing Orla needed was to pin her hopes on a relationship with a brother who didn't want to be a brother. Aislin would not see Orla hurt again. 'He didn't know you existed until a day ago. Give him time.'

When the call was done with, Aislin released an enormous breath of relief.

Whatever her doubts about Dante and his future relationship with their shared sister, the money had cleared.

That money was safe. It was Orla's.

This was no hoax or game. If they failed to convince Riccardo, that two hundred thousand would still be Orla's. When you added the DNA-dependent hundred thousand to the mix, Orla's and Finn's lives would be changed for the better, regardless of what happened at the wedding and regardless of whether Dante wanted to be a part of their lives.

Dante had done this for them.

It suddenly occurred to her that she needed to thank him.

Not giving herself time to change her mind, she

hurried off in search of the room he'd shut himself away in.

Dante was in the middle of writing an email when a knock on his office door distracted him.

His heart thumped.

It could only be Aislin.

'Come in,' he called.

She burst through the door, her beautiful face shining with a radiance the old Masters would have struggled to capture in oil.

His every sinew tightened.

Damn it, he'd finally got himself back under control, and now that control was shattered in the time it took for her to walk into his office.

He hid his discomfort. 'I'm nearly finished.'

The most captivating smile broke out on her face. 'I'm not trying to chivvy you. I just wanted to thank you.'

'For what?'

'The money has credited Orla's account. I cannot begin to tell you how happy you've made her.' She put her hands on his desk and stared at him with such force it was as if her pupils had invisible lasers pouring out of them. 'Now that I know you're a man of your word, I want you to know that I am a woman of *my* word, and that I intend to be the best fake fiancée money can buy. I will follow your lead in however you want to play things at the wedding and make darn sure that the old fool believes you and I are madly in love.'

His blood heated to imagine all the ways he could take advantage of that declaration, starting right here and now by spreading her over the table…

He pushed the heady image away with all the force he could muster and gritted his teeth. 'My only expectation is that you be you. Obviously, we will need to buy you some appropriate clothing.'

Alarm flashed in her eyes. 'What do you mean by "appropriate"?'

'Clothes appropriate for a society weekend and wedding that you feel comfortable in.'

'I don't know what would be appropriate.'

'There are stores with personal shoppers who will help and guide you. I will take you to them tomorrow.'

'Erm...' Her brow furrowed with an uncertainty he found strangely endearing. 'Are you okay to loan me the money for it? It's just that I'm skint.'

Used to women assuming he would always pick up the tab for them, it took Dante a moment to realise she was serious.

'While you are under my employ I pay for everything.' It was imperative he re-establish that this was a business arrangement and not a personal one. Imperative as a reminder to himself and the thickening in his blood and loins.

She stilled, eyes narrowing. 'So you're my boss?'

'If I'm paying you to provide a service then, yes, that makes me your boss.'

'Don't push it, Moncada.'

He narrowed his own eyes at her. 'What?'

'You're not my boss and I'm not your employee. We've come to a mutually beneficial arrangement—a quid pro quo—so please don't ruin my happy thoughts towards you.'

She had happy thoughts towards him?

That should *not* make his chest puff up.

'I did not mean it to sound so formal,' he said with a stiffness that in itself bordered on formality. 'If I have in some way insulted you then I apologise. What I meant is that you are here, in my world, at my request. My world is an expensive place to live and it is only right that I pay for the things you need that will allow you to fit into it.'

Her stillness vanished and she bestowed him with a smile of such brilliance it could have blinded him. Instead of blinding him, though, it soared through the air shimmering around her and landed in his already aching loins.

'Much better.' She beamed.

With a silent curse, he snatched his phone up and called his chef, cancelling his lunch order, then got to his feet and grabbed his jacket from the back of his chair. 'Time for lunch.'

'We're eating out?'

He gave a sharp nod. Dante could feel his control crumbling, the itch in his fingers to touch her almost unbearable.

God alone knew how he was going to survive the next five days without acting on it.

Cold showers. Lots of cold showers.

For now, he would deal with it by dining with Aislin in public.

'Do you have a favourite food?' he asked.

Her beam only widened. 'Pizza.'

When they stepped out onto Dante's street Aislin gazed up at the sun high in the cobalt sky and whipped her jumper off. She had a long black vest top underneath and the feel of the sun on her bare arms was a joy after the long winter.

As she tied her jumper around her waist, she noticed Dante looking at her as if she were a new species.

'We're not with your society friends yet,' she told him cheerfully.

'Is it not a little cold to be exposing your bare arms?'

'You must be joking. Compared to Ireland, this is basking weather. I haven't seen the sun since September.'

For all the crazy feelings surging through her, she hadn't felt this happy in years. Dante's generosity had lifted a weight from her shoulders.

The money he'd credited to Orla's account, along with the forthcoming DNA-contingent hundred thousand, would be enough to substantially better Finn's life. The extra eight hundred thousand they would receive would irrevocably change it but, for now, Aislin was thinking of more than her sister and nephew. She was thinking of Dante. She wanted to save that deal for *him*, for this man who could have thrown her out of his cottage without a cent for any of them.

They walked Palermo's cobbled streets, two of his goons three paces behind them. She inhaled all the new scents and gawped at all the new sights—the barrows of fruit and vegetables, the stalls of flowers, tables and chairs crammed on the pavements with people sat drinking coffee, many smoking, the thrum of life a beat she felt pulsating in her limbs.

'Your city is so vibrant,' she observed. 'It's like nowhere I've ever been,'

'Have you travelled much?'

'Not much outside Ireland. I've been to London a

few times and I spent a summer working in a French vineyard picking grapes but that's it. I haven't left Kerry in three years.' She grinned. 'This is very different to Kerry.'

'In what way?'

'It isn't raining for a start!' She sniggered. 'I'm doing my home an injustice. It's a beautiful part of the world and it doesn't always rain. Sometimes the sun does grace us with its presence. Our village edges a forest so you can imagine the wildlife we have on our doorstep. I remember a stag finding its way into our garden when I was about ten. Orla screamed her head off when she saw it, the wimp.'

Dante listened to Aislin's enthusiastic chatter about her home with amusement. The money crediting her sister's account had stripped the defensive, wary cloak she'd worn as swiftly as she'd stripped her jumper.

Aislin, he was learning, loved to talk.

He led her into a pizzeria, wondering how the short walk he'd instigated with the intention of exercising his desire out of him in the fresh air had backfired. Here she was, walking his streets in leggings, scuffed ankle boots, a jumper wrapped around her waist like the teenagers wore it, her hair loose and unkempt, and she was still the sexiest creature on his island. He'd had to keep his hands rammed in his jacket pocket to prevent them reaching for her.

Gio, an old friend who owned the busy pizzeria, greeted him with a warm embrace. Kissing his friend's cheeks, Dante introduced Aislin, who returned Gio's embrace and kisses as if they too were old friends, then they were led to a corner table, menus placed before them.

'Do all Sicilians snog each other?' she asked the second they were alone.

'I don't know what you mean.'

'You kissed your friend on both his cheeks. And he kissed you.'

He shrugged. 'It is the Sicilian way. We are a tactile people.'

Her eyes were wide. 'I don't know a single Irish man who wouldn't respond to a kiss by another man without a punch on the nose.'

He couldn't help himself. Dante laughed. 'You have a very unique way with words.'

'I'm Irish. It comes with the territory.' She took a large drink of the cold lager she'd surprised him by ordering.

She noticed the look he gave her. 'Don't worry, it'll be Prosecco all the way at the wedding. I won't show you up.'

'Aislin… I cannot stress this enough. I want you to be only *you* this weekend. If you want to drink Prosecco, then that's fine, but if you prefer lager then that is also fine.'

'But everyone else will be drinking Prosecco or champagne or whatever you Sicilians drink. I know you want me to be me but you're still going to have my clothing for the weekend chosen by a personal shopper—'

'A personal shopper who will *help* you, not choose for you. I want you to be able to relax this weekend and be yourself, not feel self-conscious.'

She eyeballed him for a moment then grinned and

raised her glass. 'I'm very glad to hear it. To be honest with you, grape-based drinks and I don't mix—they give me a headache.'

'Is that why you drink lager?'

'I'm a penniless student. Cheap lager is all we can afford. It's either that or cheap spirits that are as likely to contain windscreen wash in them as proper alcohol.'

Dante could not say why he found her chatter so entertaining and dragged his gaze from the wondrous lips making the chatter.

Thankfully, their pizza arrived.

Dante bit into his first slice and sighed with pleasure.

Conscious that his father's cholesterol and heart problems, which had ultimately led to his fatal heart attack, had started when he wasn't much older than Dante was now, he rarely indulged in unhealthy food, but when Aislin had ordered a spicy Sicilian-sausage pizza his mouth had watered so much he'd followed suit.

She devoured her pizza with all the enthusiasm of a starving student. But then, she *was* a student.

'I hope I'm not about to say anything insulting, but aren't you a little old to be at university?'

'Only by a bit. I had to drop out in my final year because of Orla's accident. I started my degree again in September.'

'Are you missing much by being here?'

She shook her head and took another drink. 'I'm getting the last batch of credits I need through distance learning so I can be around to help look after Finn.'

Bypassing talk about his newly discovered nephew,

he smoothly moved the conversation on. 'And you're doing something to do with history?'

'I should end up with a bachelor's degree in Medieval European history.'

'And what do you intend to do with it?'

'No idea. I wanted to be a teacher, but…' Her nose wrinkled. 'I don't think I could cope with back-chatting teenagers and all the politics. I have lost any tolerance I ever had for twaddle.'

'What was the reason for that?'

'All the rubbish I had to go through with Finn. You know he was born prematurely? Well, they had to deliver him by emergency Caesarean section. Orla was in a coma for three weeks and under sedation for around another month after that—she had massive brain trauma. She also had broken ribs, a broken arm and damage to her spinal cord, so she was stuck in hospital for half a year, then had to go to a rehabilitation place for another year on top of that. Obviously she was in no position to care for Finn, so I had to step up and be his guardian, which was not an easy thing.'

Was this where she revealed herself to be not quite as saintlike towards her family as he'd assumed? 'Because you had to give up your life?'

'No, no, because there was resistance from the authorities. I tried to get power of attorney to act for both of them but it was a nightmare. They saw this young twenty-one-year-old and thought there was no way I should be given temporary custody of a premature baby or control over my sister's finances and I had to fight them tooth and nail for it. They wanted to make Finn a ward of court.'

She waved her slice of pizza in the air as she spoke,

her indignation ripe. 'A ward of court! When I was there with him in that unit *all the time*. Three months I slept in that hospital and they wouldn't even let me name him! When Orla finally came round she was compos mentis enough to give her authority for me to be in charge of everything, but they still didn't make things easy. Honestly, the pointless bureaucracy was enough to make you weep. Whatever career I end up doing, I want it to be nothing that involves any kind of government body and nothing that involves any kind of officious stuff.'

Dante swallowed his bite of pizza down a throat that didn't want to cooperate.

He needed to learn all he could about Aislin before the wedding but this was all the stuff he didn't *want* to know and he didn't have the faintest notion why guilt weighed heavily in his chest.

When all this had been going on, he hadn't known the O'Reillys existed.

'Where was Finn's father in all this?'

'Now, there's the question.' She leaned forward as if exchanging a confidence. 'I don't know who the father is. Orla refused to say. She had some memory problems after the accident and now says she can't remember.'

He looked at her astutely. 'You don't believe her?'

'Not in the slightest. I think her memory has holes in it, but on this I'm sure she's lying, and if you ever tell her I said that I will ram a whole pizza in your mouth as punishment.'

'Are you making a threat of violence against me?' he asked, amusement bubbling so hard inside him it dampened the bile and guilt that had built up.

He wanted to ask where her mother had been during all this but held back. He didn't want to know anything about his father's old mistress and it disturbed him to think his father must have felt many of the same physical feelings towards her that Dante was feeling towards Aislin.

*Dio*, he couldn't rid himself of these damn feelings. Unfiltered and amusing, her voice flew down his ears and danced into his already aroused senses.

Lips twitching as she looked him right in the eye, she helped herself to another slice, lifted it to her mouth and took an enormous bite.

He suppressed a groan.

Aislin wasn't trying to be provocative, he recognised that much, but…

How was he supposed to concentrate away from images of making love to her in every way imaginable when he found her every movement erotic, and when every passing minute spent with her increased the ache in his loins and the heat in his veins?

And how was he supposed to take her back to his home and spend two nights alone with her under the same roof? He couldn't even rely on his staff to act as chaperones, banished as they all were to their own apartments on the ground floor, leaving him with his valued privacy…

But he could enforce some changes to their working conditions for the next few days and keep them visible.

His lungs expanded and his next exhale released easily.

That was the way to play things. They could continue getting to know each other well enough to fool

Riccardo D'Amore that they were a couple in love but always with the safety of people around them.

If he played things well enough, he would not have to be alone with her again until the time came for them to part ways.

## CHAPTER SIX

WHEN AISLIN RETURNED with Dante to his home much later that afternoon, she was surprised to find an abundance of informally dressed staff out in force cleaning the already spotless house.

'Let us have a drink on the roof terrace while dinner is prepared for us,' he said as they strolled through one of the living rooms.

The interior of Dante's house was so incredible that she was curious to see what he'd done with the roof. 'Sure, but no more coffee.'

He grinned and showed the way to a side door that led out to an external metal staircase.

The hours they'd spent in the pizzeria had flown by. Once they'd eaten they'd stayed at their table, drunk gallons of coffee and set about getting to know each other.

Dante had told her about growing up in Palermo. He'd lived in the family home in a villa by the beach but it had been in the city itself he'd felt the most comfortable, roaming in packs with his friends, all of them trying to look cool to get the girls' attention and trying to convince bar owners they were old enough to drink. He'd then explained how he'd formed and grown his business empire and his determination to break into America.

Hearing about his jet-set life and achievements only made Aislin feel inadequate with what she had accomplished, which, when you took a hard-nosed look at it, was not much at all.

He hadn't made her feel unaccomplished, though.

She'd talked of her own childhood, her friends, her closeness to Orla, her love of musicals and soap operas, her fascination with bloodthirsty medieval Europe, learning to ride a bike with her granddad before he'd died, attending weekly mass with her grandmother—all the most fertile memories of her life. Dante had listened hard, his eyes never leaving her face. She knew it was because he *had* to remember these things and not out of genuine interest but still…

What woman's head wouldn't be turned by a gorgeous man paying such attention to her?

And then she stepped onto the roof terrace and her head was turned some more.

The late-afternoon sun warm on her bare shoulders, she gazed in amazement at the magnificent view of Palermo's colourful streets and medieval landmarks. The vista before her led all the way in the distance to the glimmering sea.

Then she turned her attention to the terrace itself. Encompassing the entire roof, it contained a huge swimming pool and adjoining hot tub, a bar that would have put an Irish pub to shame, the biggest barbecue she had ever seen, a dance area and lots of seating, ranging from sun loungers to hammocks to plump sofas scattered strategically, some in the sun, some sheltered beneath beautiful wooden gazebos. Dante might be lacking a garden but there was no lacking of greenery, the terrace given privacy by encircling hedges and trees.

She could easily imagine the decadent parties he hosted up here.

Jugs of fruit juice were brought out to them, the staff member then taking a seat behind the bar, on hand for any further refreshments they might require.

'This is like another world,' Aislin said with a sigh, then nodded at a hammock tied between two palm trees. 'Can I go in that?'

Dante spread his palms. 'You don't have to ask. Do you know how to get into it?'

'Nope.'

'I'll show you.'

The elegance of his movements as he got himself effortlessly into it made her heart do a strange clenching motion, but there was no time to worry about it, because a moment later he was back on his feet indicating for her to try.

She spread her arms out to hold the rope and placed her bottom in the centre as he'd shown. Then she swung her legs round quickly, but must have got her balance wrong, for she would have toppled out of it had Dante not leapt forward to steady her.

'It takes practice.' His warm breath danced through her hair.

Suddenly she was very much aware of the heat of his body against hers, the strong arm supporting her bottom under the hammock, the chest leaning over her to catch the other side.

Aislin's grip on the hammock tightened as his scent surrounded her and filtered through her senses.

Her heart rate accelerated, all the effects strengthening when he made some adjustments and shifted her weight as if she were as light as a newborn. The blood roaring in her ears was so loud that at first she missed his instruction to lie back.

Breathing heavily, she did as she was told and had to bite back the demand that he let her go *right now*.

But then he loosened his hold and she had to bite back a plaintive wail for him to keep hold of her.

Disorientated and confused by what was happening to her, it took a moment to realise she was lying in the hammock unsupported.

Dante turned his back on her and forced air into his constricted lungs, disturbed by the heated reactions assailing him.

He drank a glass of juice slowly, gathering himself together, willing his heartbeat to regulate itself, willing his body back under control.

These reactions were the normal responses of a healthy man around a beautiful woman. It was his misfortune that this particular beautiful woman was one he could not touch.

*Dio*, she smelt incredible…

Inhaling deeply, he seated himself at the round table nearest the hammock and said, 'Tell me about your university days.'

Get them back on a conversational footing. Keep a distance between them.

Look but do not touch.

Listen. Converse. Keep a distance.

This tactic had worked in the pizzeria, proving a mostly effective way of blocking out the crazy surges of lust that kept flushing through him.

He'd been surprised by how much he enjoyed her company. Aislin had such an entertaining way with words that their time in the pizzeria had flown by.

She cleared her throat. 'What do you want to know?'

'Tell me about your friends. Boyfriends…' A thought occurred to him, one he couldn't believe he hadn't thought to ask before. 'Do you *have* a boyfriend?'

'I wouldn't be here if I had one.'

The cynical part of him almost snorted his disbelief but he held it back as he remembered that Aislin was not of his world. Her world was not motivated by money.

Aislin's world was motivated by family.

His eyes drifted back to her. She looked comfortable and secure in the hammock, ankles hooked together, russet hair spilled messily all around her head.

'I've only had one boyfriend,' she confessed, her gaze fixed on the darkening sky.

He almost snorted in cynical disbelief again. 'Just the one?'

'Yes. One boyfriend. Patrick. I met him in my second year at uni.'

'Was it serious?'

'I thought so.' There was a strange mixture of anger and defeat in her tone when she said this. 'He cheated on me.'

Dante didn't know how to respond to this unexpected confidence.

But this was Aislin and, as he'd also learned in their short time together, she said what was on her mind. His question about a boyfriend had clearly taken her mind back to the man who had cheated on her.

'He promised me the world,' she said quietly. 'I

had so many doubts about him—he was a player like you—but he convinced me I was the woman he'd been waiting for and that I was special to him. We'd been together for six months when Orla had her accident. Two weeks after it happened, one of the nurses very kindly told me that I smelt and needed to go home and get a change of clothes.'

'You spent two weeks at the hospital without a change of clothes?' Amazement at her words overrode the uncomfortable stab in his guts at her blasé way of saying her cheating ex was a player like him.

'Orla was in a coma in the intensive care unit. Finn was clinging to life in the neonatal unit. I couldn't leave. It was hard enough dividing my time between the two wards. I even asked if they could be put together but it was impossible. It was an awful time. I felt like I was being split in two. I left the hospital only once in the first eight weeks and that was to pack a load of clothes for myself. I called Patrick to come and get me, but he didn't answer, so I got a taxi home. I was sharing a house with three other women. Patrick's car was parked outside. I found him in bed with Angela.'

Dante rubbed a hand over his mouth, at a complete loss at what to say.

'He knew what I was going through.' Anger rang through the rich brogue. 'He knew I needed support. He knew my mother had no intention of coming home—she's been living in Asia for five years, and when Orla had her accident she sent a few messages, but that was it from her. All I wanted was someone to hold my hand and share just a fraction of it with me. I'd begged him to come to the hospital but he made all these pathetic excuses. In the back of my mind I knew something was wrong but I didn't have the emotional capacity to deal with it.'

'What did you do?' His question came from a throat that felt strangled, his brain whirling to think how scared and alone she must have felt.

'Told them I never wanted to see either of them ever again, shoved a load of clothes into a bag and left.'

'That was it?' He'd imagined screams and smashed crockery.

Now she twisted her head to look at him. 'I was exhausted, Dante. I hadn't slept more than a few hours in two weeks and was living on my nerves. There was nothing left in me. All I wanted to do was get my stuff and get back to the hospital. It took a long time for me to even feel the betrayal of what they'd done.'

He didn't have to imagine the devastation she'd gone through; Dante was living through his own version of it. The betrayal of those you loved was the worst of all deceits.

Aislin had been betrayed by the man she'd loved and abandoned by the woman who'd given birth to her at the time she'd needed them most.

'As cruel as his behaviour was, finding them like that did you favour,' he told her, his voice colder than he would have wanted.

He could not bring himself to say anything about her excuse of a mother.

What he knew was enough for him to know down in his marrow that Aislin must take after her father.

Sinead O'Reilly was as selfish as his own mother. It was a fine line between whose behaviour was the worst.

'How do you work that out?' she demanded.

'It meant that you knew the truth. Better than being strung along on a lie.'

'I should never have been stupid enough to believe in him in the first place. Believe me, I won't be making that mistake again. The only people I trust are my family. Well, my sister and nephew.'

'Trust no one.' He'd trusted his father. Damn him.

Dante's stomach roiled with fury but this anger was not now aimed at his lying father but at the people who'd left Aislin to deal with a burden no one should have to go through alone.

It was a misplaced anger that disturbed him.

He hardly knew Aislin. He had no reason to feel such deep fury on her behalf.

'Has there been anyone serious in your life?' she asked after an outbreak of awkward silence.

'No.' He expelled the bitterness sitting in his lungs and attempted a smile. The end result was tight on his cheeks. 'Long-term relationships are not for me. I enjoy the single life too much.'

His standard answer to questions about relationships.

He saw no need to explain himself, not to Aislin or anyone.

They needed to know *facts* about each other. Nothing more.

'If I wasn't afraid of falling out of the hammock I'd raise a glass to the single life,' she said, injecting some much-needed humour into the heavy atmosphere that had developed.

By unspoken agreement they stuck to neutral subjects for the rest of the evening.

If only he could force his body to remain neutral around her too.

* * *

Aislin dipped a cautious toe into the terrace pool and found the water heated, exactly as Dante had promised. Lowering herself into it up to her shoulders, she rested her head against the rolled side and gazed up at the night sky.

The muted city noise felt distant up here, a comforting rhythm of life, completely different from the rustle of trees and the hoots and calls of wild animals she heard when the weather was kind enough to sit outside in the evenings at home.

Ciro, the young lad who'd taken her battered suitcase into Dante's house the morning before, sat at the bar playing on his phone but his was a silent presence.

She was glad of the peace. Dante had been called out on an emergency at his father's villa just as they'd finished eating dinner. Aislin had snatched the opportunity to change into the swimsuit the personal shopper had talked her into buying that day on the off-chance she would need it that weekend.

She would never have had the courage to wear it in front of Dante.

Other than the sleeping hours, this was the first time they'd been apart since he'd collected her from his father's cottage early the day before.

The two days they had spent together had been productive and she was confident they knew enough about each other that they could fool anyone into believing they were a genuine couple. Talk came so easily to them that she had to remind herself there was a purpose behind it.

Why she had brought Patrick up, she didn't quite know. The only other person she had told about finding him in bed with Angela was Orla. Aislin had to assume it was a form of self-preservation taking control, the past rising up to remind her of the dangers a man like Dante posed.

Her growing feelings for him were inexplicable. She shouldn't have any feelings for him other than gratitude at his generosity.

Patrick had hurt her badly.

Dante was cut from the same love-them-and-leave-them mould.

But there were moments when she would catch something in his eyes that made her stomach clench and a lower part of herself melt.

It had been a relief when, after breakfast that morning, Dante had taken her to Viale Strasburgo, Palermo's designer boutique Mecca, where they had been introduced to Aislin's designated personal shopper.

Dante's unobtrusive but always present staff were a calm reassurance but nothing beat having lots of other people around and something constructive to focus on to distract the mind.

Aislin had been taken into shops where the choice and richness of what she could have had almost overwhelmed her. It had been tempting to scoop everything up, but she'd stuck to the brief of buying a minimum of four casual daytime outfits, two evening dresses, one of which should be fit for a ball, an outfit for the wedding itself, shoes and accessories and a designer suitcase to put all her new purchases in.

She still didn't understand why she'd allowed the personal shopper to talk her into buying new underwear. Her own were perfectly functional and it wasn't as if anyone would see what she wore beneath the fancy clothing. But she had gone along with it, probably out of guilt for refusing the utterly gorgeous golden ballgown the shopper had insisted was perfect for her. Perfect for a catwalk model, maybe, but not for a student from Kerry.

It made her cheeks flush to imagine Dante's face when he received the bill for it all. She knew he wouldn't begrudge buying those items, but what if the bill was itemised?

Would he imagine her wearing that underwear? And why did it make a far more intimate part of herself flush to think that?

It would be easier if he'd had any input on her clothing choices but he'd been insistent that she choose for herself without any influence from him. While she'd shopped he'd kept himself busy working on his tablet, taking her out at regular intervals for coffee and more conversation.

Three more days and this would be over, and this unwelcome longing would disappear as quickly as it had come.

Nothing could come of it. Her imagination might like to see things that weren't there but, even if the look in his eyes actually meant something, meant he had an awareness for her sexually too, she would not allow anything to happen. Dante had many excellent qualities, and she trusted him to keep his word where the money was concerned, but when it came to women he was a cad. In that respect, Riccardo D'Amore was right—Dante was just like his father.

He was not above deception either. The charade he was paying her to play her part in this weekend was proof of that. It would be a foolish woman who gave her heart to Dante Moncada…

A deep male voice startled her from her thoughts.

Aislin craned her neck to see Dante talking to Ciro.

Her heart roared in her ears as he approached her, a bottle of beer in his hand.

# CHAPTER SEVEN

AISLIN WAS FURIOUS with herself for lingering too long in the pool when she'd intended only a quick dip and fought to hide her embarrassment.

She hadn't felt an ounce of self-consciousness to be dressed in only a swimsuit with Ciro around but Dante… This was a man who had bedded many of the world's most beautiful women. Next to them she would look like a sack.

Her only saving grace was that the silvery evening light meant he couldn't see what lay beneath the water's surface.

'How are you enjoying the water?' he asked when he reached her. He spoke with a light tone but she sensed a tension in the tall, lean frame.

'It's lovely. Do you mind me using your pool? I'm sorry, I should have asked…'

'The pool is here to be used. You need to relax. These last few days have been a little…'

'Full on?' she supplied.

He nodded and took a swig of his beer.

'Did you get the emergency sorted?' she asked.

His lips tightened into a grim smile and he nodded again.

Aislin's heart clenched. He'd gone to fix something at his childhood home. He'd only buried his father three months ago.

'Do you find it hard going to the villa?' she asked tentatively.

Dante gazed into the grey eyes ringing at him with astute compassion and suddenly wondered why he hadn't taken the opportunity to stay away for a bit longer.

His father's old housekeeper had called about a water leak in one of the bathrooms. Usually he would send his maintenance man to deal with it. This time he'd gone with him.

He'd needed to escape.

Two full days with his Irish fox, listening to her lyrical brogue, watching her eat, drink, laugh, smile, frown, argue…catching a glimpse of the pain she carried in her…had built up in him.

As hard as he had tried to keep his thoughts platonic and his body in neutral, there seemed to be an override in his control where Aislin was concerned.

Her throat had moved as she'd drunk a glass of water during their dinner and the sudden urge to press his mouth to her neck had sent a charge rocketing through him that had sucked the air from his lungs. For a moment, all he'd been able to see was Aislin spread naked beneath him, a sensory image so strong he'd been on the verge of sending his staff back to their apartments on the ground floor. Only the ringing of his phone had stopped him.

Forget his teenage years. This was a hundred times worse.

He'd snatched the chance for escape, only to return

to find her in his pool. He was painfully aware that, submerged beneath the glimmering surface, Aislin wore a swimsuit.

He pulled one of the terrace seats over and ignored her question.

'Orla and I found it hard to go into our nan's home after she died,' she said softly into the silence, those compassionate eyes not leaving him. 'She lived next door to us and her home was our home. Going into it in the months after she'd died and seeing all her possession still there…it was hard. I kept expecting her to call out from the kitchen asking if we wanted a cup of tea and a biscuit.' Her lips tightened and she breathed out and smiled sadly. 'It took a long time before her death felt real.'

He took a long drink.

'It still doesn't feel real,' he admitted. 'I go in that house and I see him everywhere. He's there, and I want to talk to him, but he's gone.'

Talk to him and demand answers, starting with why the hell he'd kept a sister's existence from him.

The secret cut like the deepest of betrayals. It felt like losing him all over again.

He drained the bottle and signalled to Ciro for another, guilt that Ciro had had a date lined up for that evening adding to the combustible mix of anger and desire curdling in him.

Furious anger at his dead father.

Heady desire for the woman submerged semi-naked in his pool whose eyes were fixed on him, shadowed under the emerging moonlight.

'I always knew my father was a liar,' he said into the silence. 'He was an addict. Addicts lie. But he never lied to me. He could always come to me. I never judged him. I was his son. I knew his faults but that never stopped me loving him and wanting to help him. And now I find he did lie to me. He kept from me the worst secret a father could keep from a child.'

'Orla?'

'*Sì*. Orla. It makes me think, what else did he lie to me about? Who was the man I thought I knew so well?'

There was movement in the water as Aislin pushed away from where she'd been resting, swam to the edge closest to him and folded her arms on the side.

'Have you asked your mother about it?' she asked.

'No.' He took the fresh bottle from Ciro with a grim nod of thanks. 'If my mother knows about Orla, then that means she's complicit in the lie.'

He drank deeply and gazed into the distance, looking anywhere but at Aislin. It disturbed him that, even with the heavy weight of his mood and emotions, he could still feel her stare upon him, lasering through his skin, his body charged with awareness for her.

'Parents often lie to children if they think it's a subject they won't understand, or to protect them,' she said quietly. 'It doesn't mean your father lied to you about anything else.'

'It doesn't mean he didn't,' he snapped.

She rested her cheek on a slender forearm and sighed. 'When I think of Finn and all the struggles he'll have throughout his life, it makes my heart hurt so badly that if I could swap my body for his I would do it gladly. I love that boy and his mother so much, I don't think there's anything I wouldn't do to protect them.'

'Even lie?'

'There's many things I never thought I was capable of doing that I've since done,' she answered softly. 'It's only when you're in a specific situation that you can appreciate the depths you would go to or the heights you would climb for someone you love.'

He thought of her hovering by their beds in the hospital, alone without a change of clothes for two weeks. He thought of her fighting to be recognised as Finn's guardian and taking care of everything for both of them until her sister had recovered enough to do those things for herself.

Dante could not comprehend from where she had found her strength.

He tried to lighten the heaviness engulfing them. 'Like breaking into my cottage to get my attention?'

From the periphery of his vision, he caught a fleeting smile.

Aislin thought of Patrick. She'd been in desperate need of support after Orla's accident and who better to provide it than the man who'd promised eternal love? His reaction had been to sleep with her housemate instead.

Her mother hadn't reacted at all. Her daughter and grandson had both hovered between life and death and all she'd done was send a few text messages. Aislin didn't think she'd ever forgive her mother for that.

No one had been there for Aislin, not her friends or extended family beyond the obvious platitudes.

She'd carried the burden alone. It had been a hard knock to deal with. Unlike Dante and his declaration that no one could be trusted, she knew she could trust her sister with her life. But she would not trust anyone else again, not in an emotional capacity.

'Your father made mistakes, and I understand why you're so angry with him,' she said. 'It only makes it harder that he isn't here to answer your questions or defend himself but don't ever lose sight of the fact that he loved you. I would have given anything to have the closeness you two shared with one of my parents. My mum never wanted to be a mum. Orla and I were both accidents and we both knew it. She married my dad because my nan forced her to—she didn't want the shame of having two grandchildren born out of wedlock.'

'She sounds like a formidable woman.'

Aislin remembered the outwardly terrifying woman who'd had the softest heart with a smile. 'I adored her. Nan was the one who really raised us. She died six years ago and I still miss her.'

'What about your father?'

'He remarried and moved away. We get on well but it's hard to develop a bond with someone you only see for the odd weekend.'

Dante swallowed hard to loosen his constricted throat then made the mistake of looking at her.

The moon had risen high above them. Silver light poured down and cast Aislin in a glow.

Under this bewitching light it was too easy to sink into intimacy and spill his tortured thoughts out.

Seeing Aislin like this… It would be too easy to send Ciro away, strip his clothes off, join her in the pool, haul her into his arms and…

He'd revealed enough.

He got to his feet and drained the last of his beer. 'I'll see you in the morning. I'm going to bed.'

But not until he'd taken a cold shower.

How was it possible to have such awareness for someone when the demons in his head were so present and vivid?

It was the situation they were in, he told himself firmly as he strolled away. As Aislin had said, no one knew how they would react to a particular situation until they were in it. He and Aislin were in a strange place, thrown together and tasked with getting to know each other well enough to fool a wedding party that they were in love. That was bound to accelerate and heighten his attraction to her.

He'd reached the stairs when he realised he'd left his phone on his seat by the pool.

Cursing, he went back for it.

Dante stepped onto the terrace and strode past the bar at the moment Aislin climbed out of the pool.

He stopped dead in his tracks.

*Dio...*

A plain black modestly cut swimsuit couldn't hide a body beautiful enough to make a grown man hard on sight.

Aislin was as curvy as any man's wildest dreams.

Blood pumped furiously, pounded in him. His mouth ran dry, palms suddenly damp, perspiration breaking out all over a torso that felt as if a furnace had been ignited in it.

Oblivious to his presence, never mind the internal havoc wreaking his fully aroused body, Aislin reached down for her towel.

A groan clutched at his throat.

Only the ends of her hair were wet and she rubbed the towel gently into it then, as she spread her arms to wrap the towel around the beautiful curvy figure, she suddenly looked in his direction and froze.

Dante was too far from her to see her features clearly but even with the distance between them a charge flowed, encircling them, tightening them in its grip…

God alone knew what would have happened if Ciro hadn't appeared at that moment from behind the bar with Dante's phone.

'I was about to bring this to you,' he said, handing it to him.

Dante took it and turned on his heel.

A cold shower had never felt more necessary.

Aislin closed the zip of her new super-posh suitcase, wishing she had something to calm the butterflies playing havoc in her stomach. They weren't even butterflies, more like giant moths.

Her moonlit conversation with Dante still played in her mind but its vividness was outshone by the memory of glancing up to find he'd returned to the terrace.

The look that had been in his eyes…

The charge that had flashed through her body and raised her heartbeat… It burned her skin.

All night she'd tossed and turned, unable to settle, thoughts of Dante taking full occupancy in her mind.

The morning had brought no relief. She'd done her best over breakfast to pretend everything was fine, that she was fine, but had been helpless to stop her cheeks flushing whenever she met his gaze.

Thankfully he'd surprised her straight after by getting Ciro to take her to Palermo's most exclusive hair salon.

She hadn't seen Dante since.

She'd returned to his home and called Orla. After a long chat that had left Aislin with mixed feelings at what Orla had asked her to do, she'd donned the first of her weekend designer outfits.

When she had slid the new black lacy knickers up her thighs, she'd been helpless to stop her mind running riot, imagining Dante sliding them back off.

The days with him had found her imagination going into overdrive where he was concerned, but now she found herself helpless to stop imagining his strong body covering hers, that sensuous mouth kissing flesh that came alive with nothing more than an overactive thought.

Restless, she stood in front of the mirror again and checked her appearance for the dozenth time.

Would he think her suitably dressed for a society weekend with many of Europe's richest and most powerful people in attendance? He kept stressing how he wanted her only to be herself but she didn't want to embarrass him. She didn't want people looking at them and asking themselves what the hell he saw in her. She wanted him to be proud to have her by his side.

A loud rap on her bedroom door set her heart thumping.

Smoothing down her newly glossy hair and checking her make-up hadn't smudged—she'd used her emergency credit card to purchase a load of it after her hair had been done—she inhaled deeply and opened the door.

Dante's heart slammed into his ribs.

The slightly scruffy untamed beauty he'd last seen at breakfast had been transformed. Figure-hugging black jeans wrapped in a wide diamond-studded belt were topped with a loose striped multicoloured shirt and a smart fitted navy jacket. On her feet were unscuffed black ankle boots with diamonds running up the heels that were a couple of inches higher than her usual boots. Her hair had been cut subtly, the style the same as before but a little neater, smoother, framing her face in a way that enhanced her high cheekbones and striking eyes.

Her raspberry-coloured lips had a sheen to them, making them appear plumper and even more kissable…

'Do I look okay?' she asked with the touch of anxiety he was coming to recognise.

Realising he'd been staring, Dante composed himself. 'You look great.'

'Are you sure? You said to dress casually for the trip over. Would a dress be better?'

'No, *dolcezza*, what you're wearing suits you. You look elegantly casual.' And ravishingly sexy, he thought with an ache that went all the way through his bones.

She blew out a breath and laughed. 'That's a relief, although *elegant* might be an adjective too far. I nearly put a dress on but I'm not ready to get my legs out yet—they haven't seen the sun in years! They're so white I'm going to have to put some self-tanning lotion on them.'

'Would you normally do that?'

'No, but I'm sure all the other women there—'

'Only do it if it's what you want, and not for them. If you want my opinion, your colouring is beautiful and does not need any enhancement. Be proud of your skin as it's part of what makes you uniquely you.'

The skin he'd complimented turned the shade of a radish and it took her a beat to say hurriedly, 'Thank you for the ego boost. Before I forget, I spoke to Orla earlier. I know you've got a lot on your mind with the wedding but I promised I'd ask—she wants to know if you'll come to Finn's birthday party. She really wants to meet you.'

Thrown by the question, disarmed by the plea resonating in the grey eyes, danger ringing like an alarm in his head, Dante chose his words with care. 'Give me the details after the wedding.'

Her relief was visible. Before she could say anything further on the matter, he said, 'Before we leave, I have something to give you.'

He kept firmly to his side of the threshold.

After a restless sleep, he'd awoken full of fresh determination to keep a distance from this woman he was so drawn to.

But that look they'd exchanged under the moonlight lingered in his bloodstream. Tight arousal had sprung back to life when she'd walked into the breakfast room, russet hair tousled, eyes still puffy from sleep.

There had been the slightest jolt in her step to see him and then her cheeks had stained with colour.

Aislin, he knew with every fibre of his being, was as attracted to him as he was to her.

If she was anyone else, anyone other than Sinead O'Reilly's daughter and Orla O'Reilly's sister, he knew damn well all their long conversations would have taken place in a bed, preferably with Aislin's legs wrapped tightly around his waist.

He could not stop himself from imagining, with increasing vividness, what it would be like to be deep inside her, the colour of the hair that nestled between her legs, the weight of her breasts in his hands, the colour of her nipples…

It was a form of mental torture that he was inflicting on himself but, as hard as he tried, was unable to stop. It took every ounce of the control he'd mastered in his thirty-four years not to pull her into his arms and plunder her mouth.

But she was resisting it too and the electricity zinging between them was charged enough for him to feel it in the roots of his hair.

Her scent filled the space around them and he had to hold himself back from filling his lungs to the brim with it.

'What did you want to give me?' She was virtually rocking on her heels, cheeks still containing the remnants of her blush, eyes for once looking anywhere but at him.

'Your engagement ring.'

Now the grey eyes snapped on him. 'An engagement ring?'

'It would be strange to introduce you as my fiancée without a ring on your finger, don't you think?'

'I suppose.'

He pulled the small box out of his trouser pocket and handed it to her. 'Hopefully you will find it fits.'

She plucked it from the palm of his hand with, he noted, fingers that contained the slightest of tremors, and pressed it open.

Dante waited, chest and throat suddenly tight, for her reaction.

He'd bought it that morning. Thinking he would buy the first decent ring he saw that would pass muster under all the eyes that would undoubtedly want to look at it, he'd strolled into the jeweller as blasé as if buying a new pair of shoes.

He had not expected to walk out twenty minutes later without buying anything.

Three jewellers later he'd finally found the perfect ring for Aislin, a large pear-cut diamond encrusted with dozens and dozens of tiny sparkling diamonds, emeralds and sapphires and centred on a band of rose gold.

It was beautiful and different, just like Aislin.

It was also the single most expensive item he'd ever bought that was not bricks and mortar.

Why he had spent such an obscene amount of money on his fake fiancée he did not know, and refused to think too deeply about. It wasn't as if he couldn't afford it.

Her throat moved before she looked up and her wide, confused eyes fell on him. 'Dante, I can't wear this.'

'Why not? Don't you like it?'

'It's the most beautiful piece of jewellery I've seen in my life. If I could have asked a jeweller to make a ring bespoke for me, then this is exactly what I would go for...'

'Then what's the problem?'

'It must cost a fortune. What if I lose or damage it? You'll never be able to take it back.'

'It's yours to keep,' he said evenly.

'I can't keep it! It's too much.'

'Aislin…' He sighed and crossed the threshold, closing the gap between them enough to take the box from her hand and pull the ring out. Not giving her mouth or his brain time to protest, he took her left hand in his and slid the ring on her wedding finger.

'Listen to me,' he said quietly, moving his gaze from the ring on her finger to stare at the ring of her eyes.

Her eyes were a thousand times more dazzling.

'This is a gift from me. I already know you well enough to know you will give every cent of the remaining money to Orla for Finn's benefit, and I admire you for that. I admire much about you, *dolcezza*, and I want you to come away from our time together with something that is yours alone. Now, I ask that you do not insult me again by refusing it.'

Only when he'd finished speaking did he notice the tingling warmth on his hand and realise he'd clasped his fingers tightly around hers, and that he'd leaned his face so close to hers he could see the individual freckles on her pretty nose.

For once, Aislin had no comeback. Her tongue had rooted itself to the roof of her mouth, the pressure of his fingers around hers setting her already ragged heart off on a rampage of heavy beats.

She could smell his skin under the cologne he wore. She could feel the warmth emanating from him. If she raised the hand not being held so tightly she would be able to press it to his chest and feel if his heart was beating as erratically as hers.

Everything inside her heated and made a weird contraction, as if her body was being reset to a brand-new mode. Suddenly she was very much aware of her sensitised skin, the tight heaviness of her breasts and the surge of damp warmth between legs that no longer felt connected to her brain. Breathing became impossible.

The eyes staring so deeply into hers darkened as they inched closer and closer…

A large, tanned hand clasped the side of her neck and she caught the flare of his nostrils before the sensuous mouth she'd tried so hard not to stare at and fantasise about caught her in a hard, unyielding kiss that sent her resistance crashing.

Awareness exploded and rippled through her.

This…

His tongue flickered into her mouth, a new dark taste filling her, and then she was moulded against the contours of his hard torso. Feelings she had never known before crashed through her in a second explosion of awareness. Deep inside, the damp warmth became a furnace of bubbling need, and she kissed him back, plundering his mouth with the same intensity with which he devoured hers, all sense abandoned as her senses took full control.

It wasn't just his torso that was hard. His arousal pressed against her belly, sending a pulse of red-hot need so deep into her that she groaned from the sensation it induced.

Every part of her body came to glorious life, all dancing with heady delight to Dante's tune…

And then the dance was over.

The kiss broke and the hard body pulled away with a suddenness that bordered on cruelty.

# CHAPTER EIGHT

STUNNED, AISLIN BLINKED and tried to breathe.

Her lungs were so tight she could hardly get air into them.

For the first time she was afraid to look at him.

She was afraid of what she would see on his face.

She was more afraid of what he would see on hers.

The silence in her room was absolute.

Her legs felt so weak it took effort to make it to the nearby armchair and slump into it. She covered her mouth with her hand. Lipstick she'd applied for the first time in three years had been kissed off.

She had never been kissed like that before.

Dear God, she burned inside and out: a furnace of desire inside, intense mortification at his abrupt rejection on the outside.

Dante dragged his fingers roughly through his hair, cursing himself with all the obscenities he hadn't used since his teenage years.

What the hell was wrong with him? He'd resisted temptation many times in his adult life, mostly with wives and partners of friends who assumed his reputation meant he had no morals, and would flirt, give him the come-to-bed eyes and engineer situations at parties where they would be alone together. Beautiful, sexy women who, if they had been single, he would have taken what they were offering without hesitation. He'd resisted every one of them without hesitation.

If people were in a committed relationship then they should respect that, not go fishing for a bigger catch.

His father had had no such morals and that, until he'd discovered the existence of his secret sister, had been the only thing that had really pained Dante about him. He'd accepted his gambling addiction as an illness, but his pursuit of any female who would give him the time of day regardless of her relationship status had chipped away at Dante's respect for him.

Dante had always thought he was better than that, and yet here he was, acting on desires he'd sworn to resist. Pulling away from Aislin's arms had been one of the hardest things he'd ever done and his aching, lust-ridden body protested loudly.

When he'd gathered enough control over himself that he could at least hear himself think over the thuds of his pounding heart, he looked at Aislin, slumped in the armchair, her face in her hands.

Her back was making jerky movements.

'Are you okay?'

She slowly raised her head. 'Getting there.'

His jaw clenched. 'I didn't mean for that to happen.'

'Neither did I,' she muttered.

'I gave you my word that this deal between us would be platonic and I have broken that promise.' And that broken promise disgusted him. Damn it, he was a man of his word. 'I can only apologise.'

'Are you apologising for the kiss or for the broken promise?'

'Both.'

A flash of anger appeared in her eyes. 'I don't want it. We were both party to it and to apologise…feels demeaning.'

'I would never intentionally demean you.' He swore under his breath and sucked in a large breath of air. 'It's impossible…'

'I know. You made it clear by your actions when you pulled away that you regret kissing me; you don't need to spell it out. I might not be beautiful and sophisticated like all your girlfriends are but I'm not a complete idiot. You don't fancy me. The kiss just happened.' She jumped to her feet and put on an airy smile that was so obviously fake his heart twisted at the effort it must have taken her to make it. 'It's one of those things. Let's forget all about it.'

She went to stride past him and, without thinking, he snatched hold of her arm. 'What are you talking about?'

Her cheeks became radishes again. 'It doesn't matter. I'm being silly. I'm embarrassed, okay? You didn't mean to kiss me.'

'Aislin…' He closed his eyes and released her arm before he did something really stupid like kiss her again. He stepped out of arm's reach. 'You're right that I didn't mean to kiss you, and right that you're not sophisticated like my old girlfriends. I thank God that you're not. But you're wrong about everything else.'

There was a long period of silence then. 'What are you saying?'

'*Dio*, Aislin, have you not felt the chemistry between us?'

She stared down at the carpet. 'I thought I was imagining it.'

'Imagining it?' He could laugh at her naivety. 'Oh, *dolcezza*, no, you were not imagining it. You are possibly the most beautiful woman I have met in my life. You are loyal and funny, and sexier than any woman should be allowed to be, but I think we both know it would be foolish to allow anything to happen. Forget our family and the complications they bring, speaking only of you and me...' His mind raced ahead of him, his tongue trying to catch up on developing thoughts he realised had been there part-formed from the start. 'I'm not the heartbreaker the media portrays me as but I'm not a saint. I don't believe in love and for ever, I don't want a family and I only date women with the same mind-set. When I said you were different, I meant it. I wouldn't be good for you. You deserve better than me.'

With baited breath, he waited for her to respond.

When she finally looked back at him, there was a fire in her eyes that lasered straight through him. 'Well, I am *thrilled* you know what's best for me—it certainly saves me the bother of having to think for myself.' Then she strolled to the door, yanked it open and walked out, slamming the door behind her with a loud, 'You, Moncada, are an eejit.'

Aislin stormed all the way down the corridor to the lift and punched the button.

Heavy footsteps approached as she waited impatiently for it to reach her but she refused to acknowledge him, even when he stood beside her.

'Have you calmed down?'

'No.' She folded her arms tightly across her chest lest she punched him in the face or, worse, hooked them around his neck and kissed him.

Her awareness of Dante was so acute it muffled her indignant anger at his apology and patronising attempts to explain himself.

Had she not spent almost four days telling herself all the reasons she had to keep her desire for him locked away? she fumed.

But that had been before he'd kissed her and sent sensation flowing through her she had never imagined could exist, and before he'd said beautiful things about her she'd never been told before and then listed all the reasons why those beautiful things didn't count for jack.

That he might very well accuse her of double standards if he could read her thoughts about him these past few days only added an extra dose of frustrated turmoil to the turbulent mix eating at her.

'I've got your suitcase.'

She'd forgotten all about it.

She gave him grudging thanks.

'Am I right thinking "an eejit" is the same thing as an idiot?'

Was that amusement she detected in his voice? She refused to look at him to see.

'Yes, it is, and you, sir, are a prime example of one.'

There was a loud ping and the lift door opened.

They stepped inside and, as the door closed, she rounded on him. 'Right, Moncada, let's get a few things straight. You might be as sexy as the devil but your reputation precedes you—see? I'd already worked that out for myself because, sir, I am not an eejit.'

'What's with all the sirs?'

'They're substitutes for the names I really want to call you.' The amusement dancing in the eyes she now allowed herself to look into only made her add a few more to the choice list of them.

'Names worse than eejit?'

'Yes, sir, much worse, and I would be grateful if you would shut up so I can shout at you and get this off my chest. I resent being told what is and is not good for me. I am not a child. If I want to have an affair with you, then I jolly well will, and I would go into it with my eyes open knowing perfectly well that it would never amount to anything, and not just because you are, by your own admission, not one for anything longer term than a bluebottle's lifespan. Affairs are short-term flings, they are not a relationship. It is an insult that you think I would not know the difference.'

The lift reached the ground floor. The door opened. They both ignored it.

'I never said you didn't know the difference.'

'You implied it. All this, *"I wouldn't be good for you. I only have affairs with sophisticated women who are happy to have the end date of the relationship set before it starts"*,' she mimicked.

'I never said that either!'

'Not in so many words but that was the gist of it. Well, sir, I do know the difference between an affair and a relationship, and I also know a relationship between us is a nonstarter. My life is in Ireland with my family. Your life, when you're not travelling all over the place, is in Sicily. Never minding all the stuff with our shared sister, we are very different people culturally and morally, so why you think I would even entertain a full-blown relationship with you is, sir, an insult.'

'Have you finished?'

'No, I have not.' Frustrated beyond comprehension, and suddenly desperate to wipe the amusement from his face, she grabbed at his leather jacket to yank him to her and pressed her mouth tightly to his.

With an immediate surge of delight her body rejoiced to feel those wonderful warm, firm lips upon her again, but there was enough anger still rippling through her to ignore the delight of sensation, hold her breath and keep her mouth there for the count of three before pulling away, just as she felt his hand breezing onto her waist.

'There,' she said primly, clasping her shaking hands together and stepping out of the lift. 'Now I have finished.'

'What was that for?' The amusement had gone from his voice.

'So that I can apologise. I'm very sorry for kissing you. We made a promise to keep things platonic. I have broken it. I'm very, very sorry.'

He took the longest inhalation she'd ever heard, followed by a ragged burst of laughter.

'You still find this amusing?' she demanded.

'You would prefer me to push you back into the elevator and take you right now? Because I have to tell you, *dolcezza*, seeing as we are being honest with each other, that right now I am more turned on than I have ever been in my life.'

She squirmed as the warmth between her legs, there since before they'd shared their first kiss, heated and bubbled again, and she pressed her thighs together as tightly as she could. 'You find my insulting you a turn-on? Are you a masochist?'

Aislin thought *she* might be one. Grabbing hold of him and kissing him like that…

As her sadly deceased grandmother had been fond of saying, she didn't have the sense she was born with.

'I must be.' Dante put his hand on the exit door and blew out air. 'I keep telling myself all the reasons why I shouldn't touch you and, before you argue with me, the thing about our mutual sister is a complication that neither of us can deny.'

She made a noise that sounded like agreement.

'I need to keep a clear head to get through this weekend,' he explained heavily. 'This is the biggest deal of my life, and if we don't convince Riccardo about us then I lose it. That means I miss the profit that comes with it, miss out on breaking into America and I will lose face too, because news of the broken deal is certain to get out. I should be keeping my eye on the potential prize but all I can think about is what making love to you would be like and it is driving me crazy. Why do you think I filled my house with staff? Without people to distract us, the temptation to touch you and taste you is a battle that consumes me.'

'Is it?'

He gave an incredulous laugh. 'Five minutes alone with you without any staff in sight and I'm kissing you, so what does that tell you? That kiss blew my mind.'

She stepped to him and gazed into his eyes.

Heat pulsed through him to remember the sweet taste of her tongue in his mouth.

The succulent lips parted and her throat moved. 'It blew my mind too.'

He suppressed a groan and tightened his hold on the door handle.

'I'm sorry for overreacting,' she whispered. 'Dante, your kiss…what it did to me… I've never felt that before. It scared me—my reaction to it scared me. I forgot why I'm here and how important this weekend is to you.'

He ran a finger across a high cheekbone that flushed with colour at his touch and managed a smile he thought probably looked more like a grimace. 'Let's just get through this weekend as best as we can.'

Her shoulders rose high and she nodded.

He opened the door and they stepped into the warm spring air.

His car was parked outside waiting for them.

Aislin gaped through the car window at the sprawling concave Renaissance castle before her that made the British royal family's palaces look cheap.

Dozens of cars that even she, the least petrol-headed person around, recognised as the most expensive on the market were lined in a row to the east side of the villa, sandwiched between the beautiful cream-and-gold masonry and the towering landscaped trees.

Dante, who had surprised her by getting behind the wheel of the sleek red car that had been parked outside his home, jumped out and hurried round to open her door. He held a hand out for her.

The pear-shaped diamond ring that had so floored her with its beauty and obvious expense glittered under the high sun as she took hold of it and joined him on the gravelled grounds, so flat and even, she suspected someone must have brushed it.

She stared up at him and took a deep breath.

Green eyes bored into hers and he brought her hand to his chest. 'Are you ready for this?'

She nodded decisively and squeezed her fingers around his.

She could do this. She *would* do this.

On the drive over, he'd given her the low-down on the guests attending that he knew personally and told her in more detail what she could expect from the weekend, which basically consisted of a lavish display of wealth dressed up as a celebration. Events were kicking off with a champagne reception hosted by the father of the bride in the castle's sprawling gardens, to be immediately followed by a seven-course meal.

Neither of them had mentioned the kiss again, or where it might lead, if indeed it would lead anywhere.

It was time to get down to business and Aislin had forced her mind-set into focusing on that above all else, and it was a focus she was determined to keep.

The valet who had guided them to their parking space coughed discreetly and indicated for them to follow him inside, while another valet whisked their cases away.

As they set off, hands clasped—after all, this was show time—a two-seater sports car and a stretch limousine slowly drove past them in succession.

Inside they were led into a huge reception room where a handful of waiting staff with trays of filled champagne flutes stood discreetly, and a glamorous couple in full evening wear chatted to a small group at the far end of the room.

Aislin cringed inwardly and fought the fresh burst of panic clawing at her throat. Her casual outfit, as chic as it was, now made her feel massively underdressed.

She was never going to fit in.

'That's the bride and groom,' Dante said into her ear as they approached them.

Shivering at the brief sensation of his breath against her skin, Aislin forced a smile to her face as the couple spotted them and broke away from the group to greet them.

Alessio and Dante gripped wrists and pulled each other in to embrace tightly and exchange kisses on the cheek, the tactile Latin nature unashamedly displayed. She noted there was a slightly greater distance between Dante and the bride, who he introduced as Cristina, and then Aislin was yanked into an embrace by Alessio and an equally effusive one from Cristina. They both grabbed her hand to examine the ring on her finger.

'You're a dark horse, Dante,' Alessio said with a laugh. 'Springing a guest on us at the last minute. When Cristina said you were bringing your fiancée, I thought she had misheard you.'

Cristina flashed the whitest teeth Aislin had ever seen at her fiancé and laughed. 'One day you will learn that I am always right.'

'Don't worry, I'm learning.'

'Good!'

That they spoke in English could only be for Aislin's benefit and she was grateful to them for it, and grateful for the warmth of their welcome. She could only hope their guests were as welcoming.

After making small talk for a few minutes, Cristina said, 'I'm sure you must be keen to get to your room, so why don't I get one of the staff to show you up so you can get freshened and changed before the reception starts?'

'That would be lovely, thank you,' Aislin replied, thinking the singular use of the word *room* was a linguistic flaw. She had a pretty summer dress to change into for the champagne reception and meal.

Cristina beckoned a uniformed member of staff over and Alessio pulled Dante to one side.

They switched to their native language but Aislin sensed by their body language that they were discussing the business deal. Alessio had the look of a man apologising.

She got the chance to ask Dante a few minutes later when they followed the member of staff up the first flight of cantilevered stairs and through the warren of corridors to their rooms. Their hands were clasped again, the show of affection they needed to perform being one that didn't allow them to drop their guards for a moment.

'Yes, he apologised,' Dante confirmed. 'Alessio is ashamed of his father's behaviour.'

'I assume he's tried to change his mind?'

'He has but with all the wedding preparations Alessio hasn't been able to sit down with him and discuss it in the detail it needs. Riccardo knows that going with my competitor will give them less profit. My terms were more generous but he is proving very stubborn on the matter.'

Dante welcomed the discussion of business, a distraction from the feel of Aislin's much smaller hand in his.

He'd had to concentrate hard on Alessio's latest apology and not think about Aislin for the whole two minutes Alessio had taken him from her.

It disturbed him how much he'd resented having to let go of her hand.

This was an act they were performing. They were passing themselves off as a couple so madly in love they were going to marry. Holding hands in these circumstances was a must, but he could not understand why it felt so damn *good.*

The staff member behind whom they walked came to a stop and checked the clipboard in her arms. 'This is your room.'

'Mine or Aislin's?' he asked.

She looked again. 'Mr Dante Moncada and Miss Aislin O'Reilly,' she read, then put her hand in her pocket and removed a large set of keys, from which she carefully selected one, unlocked the door and walked in. 'Do you require a maid to unpack for you?' She indicated their suitcases set side by side by the four-poster bed.

Dante caught Aislin's furrowed, silently alarmed gaze.

'No, thank you. We will manage.'

'Where's my room?' Aislin asked the moment the woman shut the door behind her.

He closed his eyes and swallowed back the thuds of his rampaging heart. 'This is it. We've been put together.'

# CHAPTER NINE

'WHAT?' AISLIN'S SHOCKED voice echoed in his thumping head. 'We have to share? But you said…'

'That we would be given separate rooms?' He laughed morosely. 'I thought we would be.'

He heard her take a long inhalation. 'Maybe all the other guest rooms were taken, seeing it was such short notice.'

'I'm sorry.'

'Don't be.' Her own laugh was equally morose. 'Cristina probably thinks she's doing us a favour. I'll sleep on the *chaise longue*.'

'No.'

'Well you can't sleep on it—you'll never fit with those long legs.'

'I'll take the floor.'

'And get a bad back?' She opened the oak wardrobe then began opening all the drawers of the dresser.

'What are you doing?'

'Looking for spare bedding.' She muttered something that sounded like a curse then rose to her full height and raised her shoulders before facing him. 'There isn't any. We can't ask the staff for some in case it gets out and the other guests start gossiping that we don't sleep together, which will defeat every purpose of me being here. We'll just have to share the bed.'

She said it in a blasé fashion but her movements had become stiff, her gait awkward. She lifted her suitcase and put it on the bed. 'Did you want to use the bathroom before I get changed?'

Immediately his mind careered to imagining her tugging those jeans down her thighs and stepping out of them…

He replied through teeth he'd clamped together. 'No, go ahead. We've time for you to have a shower or a bath if you want.'

She shook her head violently. 'The steam will frizz my hair up and I haven't time to de-frizz it. The stylist gave me a load of stuff to put into it but I'm sure it'll take me ages to do.' She pulled out a deep red dress with pretty navy flowers patterned over it and gave it a shake, then unfolded three further outfits still encased in their protective wrapping. 'Hopefully these won't be too creased, but if they are I'm sure housekeeping will have an iron I can use.'

He had never heard her talk so quickly or avoid his gaze so much.

Aislin, he realised, was more rattled than he was about the sleeping arrangements.

Her skittishness had the effect of calming his own heightened emotions.

'If your clothes need pressing then housekeeping will do that for you.' He took the outfits from her. While he hung them in the wardrobe, she scooped a handful of lacy underwear and shoved them in a drawer, then scurried into their private bathroom with her selected dress and a large bag.

He heard the door lock and muttered a curse that he suspected was much stronger than the one she had used.

How the hell was he going to get through this?

It would be bad enough finding themselves having to share a bed even if they hadn't shared their earlier kiss but they *had* shared it and that made it all worse. Hunger was never sated by a morsel. He'd had a brief taste of Aislin and all it had done was whet his appetite.

The drive from Palermo had been torturous but they had both made a conscious effort to keep talking: about the expected guests; about the events that made up the weekend, of which the wedding itself was only a small part; about the correct etiquette, which he didn't care for, but about which Aislin had wanted to know all the details; talking, talking, talking, not another mention of that damned kiss and what it had unleashed between them.

*Dio*, he could explode from the heat coursing through him. He didn't know what to do with himself. All he wanted was to batter that bathroom door down and drag her to the bed.

Aislin slipped the dress over her head and, instead of checking her appearance, stared at the discarded clothes she'd thrown in a puddle on the bathroom floor.

How could she cope sharing such an enclosed space with Dante? Their appointed room was beautiful in both decoration and proportions but they might as well have been given an old-fashioned telephone box for all the difference it made. As soon as that door had closed them in alone, her body had come roaring back to life.

She could cope with her wild feelings for him when they were surrounded by people but when they were alone…?

She pulled hard at her hair and welcomed the fleeting pain. But it was nowhere near distracting enough to override the hot, sticky feelings rampaging through her.

She felt desperate enough to jump under the shower and set it to cold. Or call housekeeping and beg them to fill the bath with ice into which she could submerge herself.

And then what would happen? A cold shower or an ice bath wouldn't be enough. Soon their effects would wear off and she'd be back to where she was: having to share a suite with the man she desired so badly it was like a sickness had infected her.

Clenching her hand into a fist, she put it to her mouth and bit her knuckles, stifling a scream of frustration.

Desire was not supposed to *hurt*.

A knock on the door made her jump.

'Aislin? Are you okay?'

She pulled it open and found Dante standing there, a crease in his brow, the rest of his features taut.

Their eyes locked together.

Her heart thumped so hard a ripple spread through her body and lifted the hairs from her arms.

Time came to a stop. The room shrank.

Her feet rooted to the floor, her vocal cords frozen.

The green eyes she found so mesmerising pulsed. His chest rose high and then loosened jaggedly.

This sickness wasn't hers alone, she realised dimly, and as that thought whispered into her consciousness her feet bounded to Dante at the same moment he sprang to life and seized her.

One moment she was gazing at him, the next she was in his arms, like two puppets whose strings were controlled by a deity, being pulled together. Their mouths fused tightly and his tongue swept into her mouth, entwining with hers, his hot, dark taste sending sensation crashing through her.

Aislin threw her arms around his neck and held him as tightly as she'd ever held anything. His hands swept up her back, one reaching up to burrow into her hair, winding a thick lock of it in his fingers, the other roaming everywhere, while her fingers grazed through the soft texture of his thick hair and her nails dug into his scalp.

His taste, his scent, the bristles of his beard biting into her cheek, a pleasure mingled with pain in its own right…

They kissed like starving waifs given one last meal, a wet, feverish unstoppable force, and she revelled in the relief of it and moaned at the pleasure they were unleashing.

Her taut breasts crushed against his hard chest and she pressed every part of herself tighter against him. Her body was aflame with need, desperate for relief from this painful longing that had become such a part of her.

And he held her just as tightly. The strength and depth of his kisses, the hunger in them, the urgent possessive exploration of her body proved he had lost his head to the moment as much as she had.

Had *she* been possessed? Was that what this longing for him was, not a sickness but a possession?

Sickness could be cured, she thought dimly. And possession could be cured too. Sometimes the only way to cure was to purge.

Purge or not, she didn't care. What had erupted between them was a force of nature she had no intention of fighting.

They'd fought it for too long, for days that with this acute yearning growing stronger inside her had felt like for ever.

Pulling his mouth from hers, Dante burrowed his face into her neck. His beard rubbed against the sensitive flesh and he lifted her into the air to carry her to the bed.

There was no ceremony. He fell on top of her, the pair of them collapsing together, and then they were kissing again. His hand slid up her bare thigh, fingers biting into the sensitive flesh.

She tugged at his shirt to loosen it and reached for his trouser button, then lost her breath along with the use of her hands when he slid a finger under the band of her knickers and found her heat.

He groaned into her mouth before tugging at her bottom lip with his teeth.

His eyes were hooded and dilated, his ragged breaths hot on her face as his thumb found her sensitive nub, and the finger that had slipped under her knickers slid inside her.

Sensation fizzed and pulsed and Aislin writhed against him, needing more, the pleasure from his hand intense but not enough. The fire inside her blazed too hot, had burned through any inhibitions and sanity she'd had left.

She needed more. She needed *everything.*

Fumbling wildly, she found the band of his trousers again and tugged at them, desperate to free him, as desperate for his touch as she was to touch him.

And his touch showed his own manic need for her.

He muttered something she didn't understand and bit at her neck, then strong fingers were digging into her thighs and her knickers were being pulled down. She squirmed and twisted to help, wriggling them to her calves, and then kicked them away with a flick of her ankle while she finally, oh, *finally*, unbuttoned his trousers. There was not a jot of shyness as she yanked his trousers and briefs down to his hips and released him, only fevered desperation. Immediately she took him in her hand and thrilled to find him fully, hugely aroused.

She had a vague awareness of him groping for protection, and Dante's head lifting from her neck so his teeth could rip foil, and then he was sheathing himself...

And then he dove into her.

The relief was immediate and she cried out from the sheer bliss of it.

Again, there was no ceremony. Again, none was needed.

He thrust in and out of her with a driving possession that sent her senses soaring. She had never known pleasure like it and it was all-consuming.

Dante could hardly believe how hot and tight she felt and, *Dio*, how damn welcoming.

Never had he needed to be inside a woman so badly that it was like insanity had taken him over.

He pounded into her with all the madness gripping him and she matched every thrust, legs wrapped tightly around his waist, crying her pleasure, urging him on, begging him with muffled words, nails scratching through the shirt he still wore; pleading, pleading, until her neck arched, her grip around him tightened and her entire body jerked in a spasm that pushed him over the edge, and he plunged into her as deeply as it was possible to go…

And that was the moment Dante experienced an orgasm so powerful he almost blacked out.

How long that last thrust went on for, he couldn't say.

How long they lay there, Dante still inside her, still holding each other tightly, he couldn't say either.

It could have been for ever before he finally raised his head from the side of her neck to look at her.

The dazed, unanchored feeling he was experiencing was right there in her eyes.

He kissed her. Her arm slipped around his neck and she kissed him back, long and deep, razing her fingers over the nape of his neck.

And then she broke the kiss, sighed and burrowed her face in his shoulder with a jerky laugh. 'Well… that was something.'

Rubbing his chin over the top of her soft hair, a laugh escaped his own throat. 'I was thinking more along the lines of mind-blowing.'

'That works.'

Their mouths found each other again for another deep fusion that this time Dante was the one to break. 'I need to get rid of the condom,' he told her.

Her arm didn't relinquish its hold around his neck. 'One more kiss.'

He obliged, then removed her arm and disentangled himself from the woman who had given him more pleasure in one short interlude than he had experienced in the whole of his lifetime.

He could hardly credit he still had all his clothes on. All they'd managed to strip off Aislin was her knickers.

*Dio*, she had been so wet and ready for him…

The legs he walked on to the bathroom felt as if they belonged to someone else. There was a heavy fuzziness in his limbs but also a fizzing he could not explain.

He stepped back into the room to find Aislin scrambling off the bed, as dishevelled a sight as he had ever seen. The hair that had been professionally smoothed and styled was all tousled, her make-up smudged, her lips plumper than ever, bruised from his kisses.

His only-just-sated loins twitched back into awareness.

Her mouth curved into a half-smile and her eyes found his, a wariness ringing from them. 'Is this the point where we dissect what just happened?'

He leaned against the wall and folded his arms across his chest. 'Do you want to dissect it?'

She shook her head quickly and covered her mouth. Her shoulders rose up and down a number of times.

'Are you okay?'

She shook her head again, nodded then gave it another shake. She sat back on the bed. 'I don't know. To be honest, I feel a little dazed. Did that really just happen?'

He laughed, not from humour but from his own incredulity at what had exploded between them. '*Sì*. It did.'

'Dante...'

'What?' he asked.

She chewed on her lips and stared at the carpet.

He crossed the room and crouched down before her. Placing a finger under her chin to lift it, he stared into her eyes, trying to read what was in them.

Aislin swallowed hard, fighting the erratic beats of her heart, fighting the drumming in her head, but mostly fighting the crazy emotions whooshing through her body.

She had never known it could be like that.

She wanted to hook her arms around his neck, feel all those wonderful feelings for a second time and see if it was as mind-blowing as the first.

'I don't normally behave like that,' she confessed.

Now that the fire between them had been, if not quenched, then at least dampened, good old-fashioned embarrassment was snaking its way through her.

They'd both been so desperate for Dante to be inside her they hadn't even got round to taking their clothes off!

'I never thought you did,' he said gently. 'And, even if you did, there is nothing wrong with it and nothing to be ashamed of. We're both adults. We're both single.'

She managed a bluster of laughter. 'No, we're not, we're engaged.'

His returning smile didn't quite meet his eyes. 'Even less reason to be ashamed.'

'I don't want to be just another notch on your bedpost.'

His chest rose and he took a deep breath before sliding his hand around her neck and delving his fingers into her hair. 'Aislin, you could never be a notch on a man's bedpost.'

Her laugh was morose. 'You reckon? Look,' she continued, not giving him time to respond, 'I'm not saying I want anything more than this. You and I are never going to be love's young dream; we're just too different, never mind the family thing and all the complications that brings, and the fact neither of us wants a relationship, but I have to tell you… I've never had an affair before.' Suddenly realising the absurdity of the situation, she put her forehead to his and gave a genuine laugh. 'What I'm trying to tell you in my roundabout way is that I don't know the etiquette for this or how I'm expected to behave now that we've actually done the deed.'

Dante brushed his lips over hers. 'If there is accepted etiquette then no one has told me.'

'How do your lovers normally behave after you've made love?'

'Don't think about them. They are not you. You wouldn't be here if you were.'

She winced.

'Aislin, stop comparing yourself to other women.'

'But I've seen pictures of your other lovers. They're all so…glamourous!'

'Maybe, but none of them has turned me on the way you do.'

Her cheeks pinked and a spark flared in her eyes. 'Really? You're not just saying that?'

He traced a finger over her soft lips. 'You do something to me, *dolcezza*, and I am not going to apologise or feel regrets, because what we shared was incredible.'

The spark deepened into a glow and she skimmed

his finger with her pink tongue. 'It was, wasn't it? I think that's what's thrown me. I didn't know it could *be* so good.'

And neither had he.

Feeling a fresh stiffening in his trousers, Dante groaned and clasped her cheeks in his hands. 'I want to make love to you again.'

She slid her arm around his neck, pupils dilating. 'What's stopping you?'

'The time.'

'What…?' She jerked out of his hold to look at her watch and gave a squeal of dismay. 'Dante, we're going to be late! The champagne reception's about to start.'

'That's what I meant about the time,' he said with pained dryness. He stood up and winced at the ache that had set off again in his loins.

Aislin jumped to her feet and caught sight of her reflection in the full-length mirror by the bathroom door. 'Look at the state of me!'

Her unkempt hair could just about be tamed with a brush, and she could redo her make-up, but her dress was all crumpled.

'Do they have a laundry service here?' She flew to the wardrobe and wrenched the door open. 'I'm going to have to wear the evening dress I got for tomorrow night's wedding reception.'

She could scream with frustration. Tomorrow night's dress was much flashier than the one she had selected for tonight, which she had chosen figuring she should ease herself into this world gently. The only solace she could find was that, having seen Cristina's glamorous dress, tomorrow night's dress would be more fitting.

'What are you talking about?'

'I bought outfits to match the itinerary but I didn't make any allowances for the clothes being crumpled up by having sex in them.' She thought quickly as she pulled out the dress she'd bought for the wedding reception. 'How do people in your world cope with all these outfits? Why can't they just have an outfit for the wedding ceremony that they keep on for the evening party like normal people?'

'Do that, then.'

'But you said everyone will change into party wear for the evening bash.'

'No one will care if you keep the same outfit on.'

'I guarantee you, every woman will be examining my outfits as carefully as their own. I've supposedly bagged Sicily's most eligible bachelor so they're going to be extra curious about me. The clothes I wear will reflect on you.'

'I'll give the personal shopper I hired for you a call and ask her to send more dresses over.'

She pulled a face, torn between not wanting him to waste more money on her and not wanting to show him up by wearing the same evening dress twice. Aislin wanted to fit into this world for the weekend for his sake.

'I'll call her now,' he said while she stood there arguing with herself, strolling over to stand behind her and wrap his arms around her stomach. 'And don't feel guilty.' He kissed the top of her head. 'I'm the one responsible for ruining your dress and, unless you want us to be seriously late, I suggest you take your new outfit and lock yourself in the bathroom before I ruin that one too.'

* * *

When Aislin emerged from the bathroom thirty minutes later, Dante let out a whistle.

'Wait a minute before you say anything,' she ordered then hurried to her suitcase and removed a pair of jade-green high heels. She slipped her feet into them and did a twirl. 'Now you can tell me, how do I look?'

'You look like someone who had better leave this room right now before I throw you on the bed and make love to you again.' He wasn't joking.

Aislin looked ravishing. She'd showered and changed into a beautiful emerald-green silk dress that had a Roman toga appeal to it. High-necked and sleeveless, it gathered at her slender waist, where it was encircled by a thick silk band covered in hundreds of tiny crystals. Falling to her knees, it had elegance and just the right touch of glamour. In the time she'd spent in the bathroom, she'd also reapplied her make-up, her eyes now rimmed with dark kohl, giving a smoky effect. She'd cured the problem of her hair by sweeping it into a messy knot at the nape of her neck. The loose tendrils falling down the side of her face were, he was certain, unintentional. On her ears were huge hooped rose-gold earrings that suited her colouring beautifully.

'I shall assume you mean that as a compliment... *Do* you mean it as a compliment?'

'Yes. Get out.'

They'd made love but it hadn't made a dent in his hunger for her.

When he joined her a few moments later he found her backed against the wall by the door.

Their eyes met.

He wanted to haul her into his arms and ravish every part of her so badly that, right then, he was prepared to say to hell with the wedding celebrations and Riccardo D'Amore, throw her over his shoulder and carry her back inside.

She held a hand out to him.

He stared down at it. Her short but shapely nails were bare of any varnish or the ornate things he guessed every other female guest here would have done to theirs.

A pang of guilt cut through him.

He'd plucked this minnow from a small town and taken her into this city of sharks he inhabited. Even if Riccardo failed to be convinced that Dante was a changed man who was nothing like his deceased father, he had a duty to take care of his minnow and keep her safe from the predators who would eat her alive.

He would not let her out of his sight.

# CHAPTER TEN

UNIFORMED STAFF WAITED at the bottom of the stairs to lead the guests through the castle to the champagne reception outside.

Her hand firmly clasped in Dante's, Aislin gazed in awe at the enormous rooms with their high frescoed ceilings and ogled the furnishings that were a mix of old and new, gaudy and stylish. She guessed the generations who had lived here had simply replaced curtains and carpets when the old ones were worn with the latest trends and without sympathy with what was already there. The lack of internal uniformity turned what could easily have been an imposing monument into something more relaxed.

She tried to compose her features into something more relaxed too.

Beneath the beautiful dress she wore with its expensive price tag, she was painfully aware she was just plain old Aislin O'Reilly, a small-town Irish girl whose most glamorous wedding invite to date had been in a three-star Dublin hotel.

A hugely obese man stood on the patio area by the wide double doors that led out to the beautiful gardens, holding court and greeting the guests as they were brought outside.

'Is that Cristina's father?' Aislin asked in an undertone.

'No. That's Riccardo.'

'I thought Cristina's father was hosting this reception?'

'He is but Riccardo cannot resist muscling in and taking over. He has to be in charge even when he isn't.'

'And you want to do a business deal with him?'

'No, I want to do a business deal with his son.' He squeezed her hand, indicating this whispered conversation was over because now they were being taken to him.

Riccardo greeted her politely enough with the traditional Sicilian embrace and kisses, but then took hold of her hand and peered down to examine her ring.

'You are to be married,' he said in heavily accented English when he finally released her, and focussed his little piggy eyes on Dante. 'Congratulations.'

From the tone of his voice, Aislin guessed he already had suspicions about the authenticity of their relationship.

'Thank you,' Dante replied smoothly.

Riccardo patted his perspiring forehead with a handkerchief. He looked as if he was about to say something else when a tiny middle-aged woman with short hair, wearing a trouser suit, joined them.

Immediately, his whole demeanour softened.

'My wife, Mimi,' Riccardo said, before addressing his wife in Italian.

Mimi fixed keen eyes on Aislin before embracing

her and kissing her cheeks. 'No English,' she said, waving her hands as if in apology.

'No Sicilian,' Aislin replied with a grin. Although Sicilians mostly spoke their own dialect which to her untrained ear sounded just like Italian, her studies had taught her that Sicilians were proud of their island and proud to call themselves Sicilian.

Dante spoke a few more words and then he led Aislin away from the D'Amores to join the glamorous guests milling around over the immaculate lawn.

'Don't leave me,' she whispered, squeezing his fingers in her anxiety.

'I won't. Relax.'

And then she found herself thrust into the heart of the crowd which ranged in age from small toddlers right up to a wizened old man with an oxygen tank attached to his wheelchair.

Names were thrown at her, embraces and kisses exchanged and an ever-replenished stream of champagne and fruit juices carried by model-pretty staff was readily available.

When Dante introduced her as his fiancée, virtually everyone found it impossible to hide their shock. As he'd predicted, everyone was keen to look at her engagement ring, and the women especially made appropriate cooing noises.

But she also noticed the whispers between them and the side glances, and felt herself being weighed up and judged. Not all the judgements were favourable. One woman in particular, a beautiful sloe-eyed brunette called Katrina, gave her the chills. Aislin knew she was prone to an overactive imagination but the Medusa had had a friendlier stare than Katrina.

Dante kept her hand in his protectively throughout, as if he were an anchor keeping her rooted through her navigations in this mega-rich world.

It took half an hour of awkward social chit-chat before people stopped feeling the need to circulate quite so extensively and formed small groups. And that was when she received her first real line of questioning.

'How did you two meet?' asked a tall, willowy blonde called Sabine who had mercifully kind eyes and a small child clinging to her legs. Aislin was pretty sure she recognised her and thought she might have once graced the covers of the glossy magazines her old treacherous housemate had liked to buy. Sabine's husband, a squat French media tycoon, had excused himself for a cigarette.

With the Medusa woman finally out of her eyeline, Aislin lowered her guard. 'I broke into his father's cottage and tried to attack him with a showerhead,' she answered with a grin.

Clearly thinking she was joking, Sabine laughed. 'That's one way to make an impression.'

'She certainly got my attention,' Dante drawled, thinking Aislin had pitched her answer just right.

'I can see that. And why did you break into his father's cottage?'

'Ah, well, this is where it becomes a little tricky to explain.' She took a small sip of the champagne she was nursing. 'We share a sister.'

Sabine's eyebrows shot up so high they almost met her hairline.

Dante listened to Aislin explain in that humorous, lyrical way of hers the bare facts of their circumstances. She managed to convey it all without laying blame on anyone and by making it seem, without saying the actual words, that it had been inevitable that they would fall in love.

If he didn't know the truth, he would have been convinced himself.

Sabine turned her attention to him. 'Have you met Orla?'

'Not yet,' he told her smoothly, not adding that he had no intention of meeting her.

A tightness cramped in his guts. He'd given a deliberately non-committal answer to Aislin's invitation to Finn's party. He should have given a firm no.

When this weekend was over his life would return to normal and he would forget all about this sister he'd never known existed and had managed perfectly well without. He would have given her enough money from his own funds that he need not feel any more needless guilt.

And he would forget about Aislin too. If she ever became in desperate need of money, she had the ring. She could sell it and find it worth more than the money Orla would get from Aislin's pure-hearted generosity.

They would all be taken care of and he would carry on with his life.

For this weekend, though, he would take full advantage of the time they had together.

His vow to keep his hands off her and keep things platonic between them had been broken—and, *Dio*, *how* it had been broken—and he had no intention of denying himself more of the exquisite joy he'd found with her.

Dante pulled his gaze away from his Irish fox, now talking with real animation to Sabine about Italian medieval history. Dante had known Sabine for years. He'd steered Aislin to her as, of all the women there, she was the most likely to take her under her wing and not treat her as a rival.

He sensed Riccardo's stare on them and the curiosity behind it. Everyone here was curious about Aislin.

He thought of Lola and the women who had come before her. Forget discussions of medieval history, they would have been too threatened by Sabine's beauty to delve any deeper than a fake tribute to her outfit. They would have been friendly enough but their claws would have been primed, ready to strike at the first sign of weakness, anything to make a perceived potential rival feel small. Aislin had none of that cattiness.

She had a temper on her, though. *Dio*, she had fire in her soul that matched the russet of her flame-like hair.

A huge brass gong was brought out to the grounds, its clang ringing through the still spring air.

Dante breathed a sigh of relief. That was the champagne reception done with. Now it was time for dinner.

In a few hours he would make their excuses and take Aislin back to bed.

The dinner was held in the sumptuous banquet room and the food they were served was delicious and befitting a castle of this magnificence.

Close to a hundred people were seated around a horseshoe-shaped table and it made Aislin's brain hurt to think double the number would be arriving tomorrow for the wedding itself. As Dante's guest, she was on the special insider list of guests which consisted of close family and the closest of friends chosen to spend the whole weekend with the happy couple.

A waiter appeared at her shoulder with a fresh cocktail for her. When they had first filled everyone's wine glasses, Dante had discreetly asked if she could be served something different. Feeling it would totally lower the tone if she had a beer, she'd asked the waiter to come up with something for her. The result was a colourful fruity cocktail that tasted divine. Thankfully, Katrina the Medusa was at the furthest end of the table to her and out of her eyeline, enabling Aislin to relax.

Dante was more relaxed than she'd known him too.

Making love had changed the tone of their relationship. The desire that bound them in its grip had revealed itself in glorious colour. There was nothing left to hide.

Over the seemingly ordinary words they exchanged throughout the meal ran an undercurrent, a seduction, every catch of his eye making her pulse jump, a heady promise in the air of what was to come when this meal was over. Electricity zinged between them. She could feel it as clearly as the beats of her heart. The heat of his thigh pressed against hers lasered through the material of her dress, the effect the same as if she were naked.

She yearned to see him naked.

How many courses had they had? Five or six? She'd lost count.

Lifting her glass to her lips, she took a long drink and put it back down with a trembling hand.

Dear God, she was shaking.

She managed to breathe a little easier a moment

later when the efficient serving staff filed back in and laid individual hot chocolate puddings before them all.

Aislin cut into hers and watched the thick chocolate goo spill out.

That chocolate goo was her, she realised helplessly. Inside she was melting for him.

It was the most delicious dessert she'd ever tasted but she struggled to swallow even a small mouthful.

'It's not like you to leave food,' Dante murmured when she put her spoon down and pushed her plate aside.

She looked into his eyes and searched desperately for a witty retort.

No retort came, only the truth. 'This is your fault.'

He leaned closer so his warm breath whispered against her earlobe, 'What is?'

She turned her face slightly so the tip of her nose brushed his cheek and inhaled his musky skin. 'That I've lost my appetite for food.'

'Do you have an appetite for something else?'

It took all her strength not to dart her tongue out and lick him.

She clenched the insides of her thighs, as if that action would be anywhere near enough to reduce the heat swirling and pulsing in her pelvis. Every cell in her body danced with awareness…

'Enjoying the dinner?'

In the flash of a moment Aislin was pulled back to earth.

She turned her head to Riccardo D'Amore, who stood behind them, well aware she was blushing like a teenager.

She forced her attention away from Dante's hot

body and the things he was doing to her to the here and now.

Riccardo had made a beeline for them during this sumptuous meal, giving them an excellent opportunity to seal the validity of their relationship in his mind and for her to charm him for Dante's sake.

Unfortunately, she didn't have a clue how to charm *anyone*, and reminded herself that Dante only wanted her to be her. Which was just as well, seeing as she didn't know how to be anyone else.

She would have to blag it.

For Dante's sake she would blag it to the best of her ability.

'Yes, thank you,' she answered cheerfully. 'The food is divine and there's so much of it! I'm just sorry I stuffed my face in the earlier courses because I'm too full to manage another bite.'

Dante put aside his irritation at the interruption and listened with the utmost bemusement at the chatter falling from Aislin's lips. Turning to Riccardo, he was further bemused to see something close to adoration spread over his jowly face.

'The food please you?' Riccardo asked, moving his bulk between them.

Dante could have stuck his spoon in him for forcing Aislin's thigh to part from his.

A rush of discomfort zapped through him to acknowledge that, far from welcoming Riccardo's interest in them, which was the whole reason he was paying Aislin such an obscene amount of money, he was having to bite his tongue to stop himself from telling Riccardo to get lost and leave them alone.

'It's better than any restaurant,' she enthused. 'And the cocktails are to die for. Have you tried one?'

'No.'

'Here.' She handed her cocktail glass to him. 'Try that. I haven't used the straw, you're safe.'

Dante did not think his bemusement could grow any more than to see Riccardo D'Amore complying with Aislin's order.

He took a sip and pulled an appreciative face. *'Molto bella.'*

She obviously got the gist of his approval for she beamed. 'I don't know what it's called—the waiter made it for me.'

He grinned in reply then looked from Aislin to Dante. 'You share sister?'

Needles made a sudden sharp crawl up Dante's spine.

So this was why Riccardo had come to them. The Sicilian gossip mill was on excellent form that evening.

Aislin answered for them with a proud nod and reached into her little clutch bag. 'Her name's Orla. Do you want to see a picture?' She scrolled through her phone and thrust it at him. 'That's Orla.'

Riccardo looked from the picture to Dante, his eyes as black as night. 'She look like your father.' The gist was clear—here was proof of Salvatore Moncada's amorous, immoral ways from beyond the grave.

Dante inclined his head in acknowledgement. The needles had made their way to his scalp.

Aislin took her phone back and scrolled again. 'That's Finn, Orla's son. He's an angel.'

Riccardo smiled. 'A beautiful boy.'

'He is!' she agreed with enthusiasm. 'And he's as bright as a button. He's got cerebral palsy, but he never lets it get him down, and he's always so happy. It's such a shame Dante's missed out on the first three years of his life but obviously that's not his fault, considering he didn't know Orla or Finn existed until recently, but that's all changing—he's buying them a house and is going to help as much as he can. I know he's going to make a fantastic uncle.'

'And father?' he asked pointedly after a beat that was probably caused by him struggling to keep up with Aislin's lyrical flow of chatter.

'One day,' she replied before Dante could get a word in. 'We want to enjoy married life first before having children.'

She made it sound so natural. So real.

He should be proud that she was sticking so closely to the script they'd created but all he felt was those damned needles digging into him.

Oblivious to Dante's darkening mood, Riccardo said, 'You know when you marry?'

'We only got engaged last week.' Aislin spoke if she were confiding something of tremendous importance. 'We're thinking the end of summer—that should give us time to plan it all. We've already decided we want a big white wedding and there is so much to do for it… Well, you would know all that; I bet this weekend's celebrations took months to prepare.' She fixed him with a look that conveyed she held Riccardo responsible for all the planning that had taken place and that she thought he was amazing for having done so.

'It took lot of planning, *sì*.' He nodded, puffing up like a peacock spreading its plumes.

'We'll have to pick your brains about it.'

'It would be my pleasure.'

She beamed again.

Riccardo finally gave his attention to Dante. Switching to their own language, he said, 'I'm impressed. When you get bored of her, send her to me. I have a nephew who would love her. It's time he settled down.'

'Aislin is not a chattel to be passed around.' Dante clenched the stem of his glass to prevent himself from jumping to his feet and knocking Riccardo off his.

The older man stared at him levelly but with a sneer forming on the side of his face. 'I'm glad to hear you say that but I will believe it when I see it. You've treated all your women before her like chattels. But then, they always treated themselves like a commodity too. This one is different. Look after her.'

Then he leaned down, kissed both of Aislin's cheeks and shuffled back to his seat.

Dante drained his wine and fought the swelling urge growing like a tempest inside him to smash the glass on the table.

Sensing danger, Aislin placed a tentative hand on Dante's thigh. She propped her elbow on the table to rest her chin on her free hand and gaze at him. The tension she'd sensed in him on his roof terrace the night before had returned.

'What did Riccardo say to you?' she murmured.

'Nothing important,' he dismissed with a quick smile.

'Then why have you got a face like thunder? Did your plan backfire? Did he not like me?'

'He liked you.' He gave a muted laugh. 'He said

that, when I get bored of you, to pass you on to him so he can marry you off to his nephew.'

Her nose wrinkled. 'Ew.'

She didn't get the chance to question Dante any further for a chill snaked up her spine and the willowy figure of Katrina appeared, talons holding her champagne flute tightly.

'If it isn't the happy couple,' she purred, sliding into the space Riccardo had vacated.

'Do you want something, Katrina?' Dante posed his question politely but there was an edge to his voice.

'I'm just concerned for your fiancée.' She fixed hostile eyes on Aislin. 'It's so hard to be an outsider at an event like this. Are you finding it very difficult?'

Aislin tried not to let her intimidation at the underlying malice behind the seemingly kind question show. 'Everyone has been very welcoming.'

'That's Sicilian hospitality. No one would *dream* of saying anything cruel to your face.'

'No, they would rather make petty remarks to make them feel small,' Dante cut in, his contempt undisguised. He got to his feet and took Aislin's hand. 'Go back to Giovanni, Katrina, and leave Aislin out of your games. *Buona notte*.'

Confused at this short confrontation, Aislin let him lead her out of the banquet room, her mind racing at the why of what had just happened.

# CHAPTER ELEVEN

AISLIN WAITED UNTIL they walked the deserted corridor towards their room before asking, 'What was that about?'

His features were taut. 'Katrina playing mind games.'

'Why would she do that?'

'She's a bitch.'

'Is she an ex-lover of yours?'

'No.'

'Does she want to be your lover?'

He unlocked their door. 'Yes.'

For a moment Aislin thought she was going to be sick. 'Is that why she hates me?'

Dante saw the colour fade from Aislin's face and sighed as he shut the door. 'She hates any beautiful woman. Katrina used to be a model. She married an Italian film producer thirty years older than her, thinking it would turn her into a star, but she has no talent. She's bored and stuck in a loveless marriage and gets her kicks from sleeping around. She's a predator. This is the world I live in, *dolcezza*. It's filled with people who care only for their own pleasure and advancement.'

Having Aislin on the receiving end of the bitchy comments that usually passed him by...

The protectiveness he'd felt towards her…

He tugged his jacket and tie off and threw them on the armchair in the corner of the room.

Riccardo's observation about Dante's past lovers had been accurate. His experience of women being all the same was because he had deliberately gone for women of the same mould as each other. He had seen in them what he had wanted to see and it had suited them to play along with it.

Katrina was of that mould. The only thing that had stopped him taking her as a lover was her marital status.

He cradled Aislin's cheeks in his hands and gazed into the striking grey eyes.

She was everything Katrina and the lovers of his past weren't.

Aislin was beautiful inside and out.

He brought his mouth to hers and inhaled the sweetness of her breath before claiming her with his kiss.

It was the mind-blow he needed.

Her scent, her arms locking around his waist and the receptive parting of her lips all worked together to drive out the demons Riccardo's words had dredged in him.

Dragging his fingers across her face to burrow into the knot of her hair, he fought his body's wild response to devour her as quickly as possible.

This time he was going to take it slow.

This time they were going to do it properly.

Splaying his fingers, he found the pins holding her hair in place and pulled them out.

Her russet locks fell in a messy tumble over her shoulders. He rubbed his nose into it and inhaled the scent of raspberries.

As he found her lips again, a distant thought told him he would never again see or taste his favourite fruit without thinking of Aislin and remembering the colour of her lips and the smell of her hair.

Her hold around his waist tightened and she pressed herself so closely to him not even a sliver could come between them.

Dante rubbed his hands down her arms and took her hands in his. He led her to the bed and sat her down, then gently parted her legs to kneel before her.

Like this, they were of equal height.

Gazing into the eyes he felt certain he could pick from a thousand others of a similar shade, he unbuttoned his shirt and shrugged it off, letting it fall to the floor beside him.

Her eyes widened and pulsed.

She reached a trembling hand and placed it to his chest.

He closed his eyes at the sensation her touch released in him.

Aislin could feel the thuds of his heart against her palm and felt the strangest urge to cry.

That was Dante's heart beating so heavily for her. His smooth brown skin covered in dark hair that was softer than she had imagined, his brown nipples, his defined pecs, his taut abdomen.

This was him.

He was beautiful.

Slowly she caressed her fingers over him, soaking it all in with her touch and her eyes. She leaned closer and inhaled the musky scent of his skin and the overlaying spicy cologne. It was a dreamy combination that dived straight into her veins.

Then she continued with her fingertip exploration, dancing lightly down to the belt of his trousers.

Lifting her eyes to stare into his, the hunger gazing back at her knocked the air from her lungs.

She drank his potent hunger in, then leaned forward to press the lightest of kisses to his slightly parted mouth. Aislin closed her eyes and breathed in the scents she found. Coffee, liqueur and Dante himself all coiled like an invisible vapour to join the traces of his skin already committed to her memory and snaking deep in her bloodstream.

She tugged at his belt and kissed his neck. She tasted something indefinable. Dante.

When she finally had the belt undone she found the button of his trousers. As before, she struggled to undo it but there was no rush. Whereas earlier their pent-up desire had erupted and taken them on a soaring supercharged roller coaster, now there was a feeling of calm, as if they had all the time in the world to do all the things they had both dreamed of and fulfil all their unspoken desires.

These were desires that only a week ago had not existed in her.

A week ago, she might as well have been dead from the waist down. Sex and intimacy had had no meaning to her.

The tilting of her world and her awakening to desire no longer frightened her. Dante's reputation no longer frightened her. Even the whispered thought that she would never have these feelings for anyone else didn't frighten her.

If all they had was this weekend then it would be enough.

He leaned forward and brushed his cheek beside hers. His hand rested on hers and together they undid his button and pulled his zip down.

Then he kissed her neck and rose to his feet.

His chest rose sharply as he gazed down at her before removing his trousers and underwear to stand before her, fully, magnificently naked, erect in all senses of the word.

Her thundering heart twisted and her core pulsed and contracted.

Dante was beautiful. Every part of him.

'I want to see you,' he said thickly.

Keeping her eyes on his, she unbuttoned her dress at the neck and removed the crystal-studded belt. Then she lifted her bottom to ease the skirt of the dress up to her waist and pulled it up and off over her head.

She flung it away, uncaring where it landed.

All she cared about at that moment was Dante.

When she next looked at him, what she found sent a rush of emotion ripping through her. His jaw was clenched, his eyes hooded. His breathing was as heavy as the thuds of her heart.

If she'd had any fears about being naked before him that look would have blown them away.

But she had no fears. They had already been blown away.

She reached her hands behind her back and unclasped her bra.

The relief in her breasts to be freed from the lacy restriction was a pleasure in itself, but only a fleeting pleasure, because the ache in them suddenly came into sharp focus. They felt so *tight* and heavier than she had ever known them to be.

But the look in his eyes now was exhilarating.

Slowly she lifted her bottom again, this time to pinch her knickers and pull them down, shaking them off with her feet so that she was as naked as he, and the anticipation of what came next reverberated through her very being.

For the first time in his life Dante was scared to touch a woman, afraid that to touch would be to lose his head a second time.

Every inch of him strained towards her, every inch of his flesh attuned to her frequency. His heart beat so loud and so hard his chest hurt from the blows.

Naked, she was more beautiful than anything his feeble imagination had conjured.

Milky-white skin that looked as if it had never seen the sun set against the almost violent contrast of the deep russet of her pubis. Plump, wholly natural breasts topped with taut nipples the colour of raspberries…

*Bellissimo.*

Using all the restraint he could gather, he stepped towards the bed and placed a knee between her thighs, then gently eased her down so she lay flat.

He hovered over her for a long moment with his hands placed on either side of her head and did nothing but stare at her beautiful face.

She gazed back.

And then he crushed her lips with his mouth and the rush of desire broke free to consume him.

He kissed her everywhere. He explored her beautiful milky body with his mouth and his hands. He discovered all her tastes and scents, devoured her breasts with his mouth and discovered a flick of his tongue over the raspberry nipples made her gasp. Lower down and he discovered a new heady taste and scent, and discovered a flick of his tongue over her swollen nub made her cry out. When he kept his face there and slid a finger inside her…*Dio*, he had never known such wet heat was possible…he learned even more of her secrets.

And then she learned his.

One minute she was on her back, the next she'd wriggled out from under him and had *him* pressed down on the bed, and then she was covering his body with her mouth and touch, making the same explorations. He could feel the wonder and delight in her movements and for the first time in his life felt as if *he* were being made love to.

Aislin had passion in her pores and fire in her soul, he thought dazedly, and when he was finally sheathed and sliding inside her his last coherent thought was that she was the perfect fit for him.

Aislin's mind had gone, slipped away. All that was left of her were nerve endings.

Dante's cheek was crushed against hers, his body crushed on top of her, driving in and out of her, and the *pleasure*…

It was like nothing she had known before.

She had thought their first time could never be beaten but this…

This was everything.

If the good Lord should come for her now, she would go with rapture in her soul.

The tempo of his love-making increased and she adjusted with it, and as she did so the pleasure heightened.

Words tumbled out of her mouth, an incoherent jumble of cries for more, pleas for this never to end, never end, never end…

And then the words were sucked out of her as the pleasure reached its peak and exploded. She cried out at the same moment Dante released an animalistic roar that penetrated through her skin.

Waves of release crashed through her and she clawed at him, sobbing into his damp cheek pressed so tightly to hers, riding the glorious surges for as long as she could until her entire body felt saturated with their flow.

It was a long time before she could breathe with any semblance of normality.

Blood pounded in her head, pounded in every part of her satiated body.

Eventually Dante lifted his head and kissed her with a tenderness that filled her heart before gently moving off her.

She watched him walk to the bathroom and was suddenly overcome with another urge to cry.

Where the tears came from, she couldn't begin to think, and she blinked them away, burrowing under the covers, not wanting Dante to see.

But it had been beautiful.

When he slipped under the covers beside her and hauled her into his arms, she had to bite her tongue to stop words she would regret in the morning from being spilt.

There, in the darkness, lying with Dante in a jumble of limbs, the urge to say that she loved him almost overwhelmed her.

Aislin crept out of bed and slipped Dante's discarded shirt on. It smelled of him.

She gazed at his peaceful sleeping form with a lump in her throat. An arm was thrown over his head, the sheets tangled around his waist, his breathing deep and regular.

She took her own deep breath and wrenched her eyes away from him to pad to the coffee machine on the table at the end of the room. Once it was made, she took the cup and her phone out onto the secluded balcony, leaving Dante to sleep. The Lord knew he needed it.

There had not been much in the way of slumber that night.

She should be shattered herself but instead she felt wired.

And scared.

She took a sip of the coffee and stared over the balustrade, desperate to shut her thoughts down before they could gain traction.

The only sound was the early-morning bird call. It was so early she doubted even the children were awake.

There was a chill in the early-morning air but the brightening sky was cloudless and promised warmth. The sea in the near distance—she hadn't realised how close to the shoreline they were—had hardly a ripple in it.

She gazed wistfully at it, wishing for the same calm to replace the ripples of tension within her, then scolded herself for even acknowledging it.

She'd known what she was doing last night when she had made love with Dante. These feelings were nothing but a side effect of the heady hormones that had taken her in their grip.

*But you never had these side effects with Patrick...*

She dismissed that thought immediately. Compared

to Dante, Patrick had been a child, and the girl whose head had been turned by the university jock didn't exist any more.

Dante had awoken the woman inside her. And, unlike with Patrick, she had gone into this affair with her eyes open. Dante had no power to hurt her.

The jealousy she'd felt when she'd fleetingly suspected Katrina of being one of his ex-lovers had been an irrational reflex. Nothing more than that.

The warmth that had filled her at his protectiveness towards her then was nothing but a reflex too.

Needing to take her mind off him, she put her coffee on the table and called her sister. Finn's needs meant Orla had to get up early to care for him.

'What are you doing up at this god-awful time?'

Her sister's rude greeting soothed her.

This was familiar territory.

'I'm standing on a balcony looking over the Mediterranean Sea.'

'Is it raining?'

'There isn't a cloud in the sky. How's Finn?'

'Watching television. He's only asked about you twice since he got up. Have you spoken to Dante yet about his party?'

There was such hope in her sister's voice that Aislin's heart twisted. Poor Orla, let down by so many people: their mother, Orla's father, Finn's father, whom Aislin believed must have let her down in some way for her to have kept the pregnancy from him… All this heartache and still Orla longed for a relationship with the brother she'd never met.

Aislin would do anything to protect her sister and

Finn and it was with a sizeable lump in her throat that she confirmed Dante was hoping to make the party.

She had to trust him on this…

It came to her that she *did* trust him on this. She trusted him enough to let him into her sister's and nephew's lives. Trusted that he wouldn't let them down and hurt them like everyone else had.

It wasn't just the intimacy Aislin had shared with him, or their moonlit talk where they had opened up properly, but a combination of it all.

Orla's happiness at this was infectious, lightening Aislin's mood right until, a few minutes later, she asked, 'Are you still coming home Monday?'

Aislin's heart made a sudden wrench.

'If I can get a flight.' She hadn't even looked at the flight schedule.

Whatever flight she got back, she still only had one night left with Dante.

How quickly things turned on their head.

The slide of the patio door made Aislin turn *her* head.

While Orla started to go into detail about the wheelchair-friendly car she was thinking of buying, Dante, who'd thrown a pair of shorts on, came to stand behind her. He wrapped his muscular arms around her waist and placed a kiss on the top of her head.

Her wrenching heart broke off into a thundering run.

'What colour are you thinking of?' she asked inanely, then missed the answer because Dante had pressed his groin into the small of her back.

He was already fully aroused.

Aislin strove to keep a grip on the conversation but it was a losing battle. Dante slid a hand up her—his—shirt. A large hand found her breasts and squeezed, the other tugged at her hair to tilt her head back, exposing her neck for him to raze his tongue over.

The heat he ignited was instantaneous.

And then he spread his hand down her belly to her bare pubis.

She already knew she was ready for him.

When he slid a finger inside her, he knew it too, and gave a muffled groan into her hair.

'What was that?' Orla asked.

'Room service,' she lied, straining to keep her voice even, but too aware that Dante was tugging his shorts down.

He rested his length between her buttocks and ground into her.

Her entire abdomen melted into lava.

Then came the sound of teeth ripping foil.

'I'd better go,' she said, aware her voice must sound shaky but no longer having any control of it.

Dante pressed her forward and gripped her hips.

'I'll call you back later. Love you, bye.'

Then she disconnected the call at the same moment Dante entered her.

His love-making was fast and furious, an elemental force that released something new, something primal, in her.

When it was over and she stood gripping the balustrade, weak-legged and throbbing from the carnal pleasure he had unleashed, he gently pulled her hair back again and twisted her head to kiss her.

'What are you doing to me, *dolcezza*?' he asked with a groan into her mouth.

She laughed weakly. 'What are you doing to *me*, more like?'

His own laughter was shaky. 'I have no idea how I'm going to get through this day without dragging you off somewhere to make love to you.'

He disappeared back into the room to add to the growing number of condoms in the bin. Aislin picked up her phone, dropped from her fingers without her remembering, and wondered how the heck she was going to get through the rest of her *life* without making love to him.

## CHAPTER TWELVE

DANTE DROVE THE short route to the cathedral. Normally he loved to be behind the wheel. When it came to getting from A to B in his busy daily life, he preferred to be chauffeured. Time was a premium. Being driven meant he could get on with work.

As this was a weekend for pleasure he'd decided to drive himself but now regretted the decision. He had to concentrate hard, and fight his eyes from staring at Aislin beside him, ravishing in an off-the-shoulder figure-hugging navy blue dress.

His awareness for her had become a burning infection in him. It consumed him.

When they'd joined the other guests for breakfast, he'd had to remind himself that holding her hand was for show.

But that had been a lie to himself.

It had been such a natural thing for him to do that he hadn't even realised he was holding it until they'd entered the banquet room and he'd been forced to let it go.

Once they'd finished breakfast, she'd gone up to their room, ordering him to give her an hour before joining her so she could get ready for the wedding in peace.

He'd known exactly what she meant. After their escapade on the patio, which his loins still burned to remember, they'd taken a shower together and got so carried away they'd come within a breath of not using a condom.

To while the time away, he'd played snooker in the games room with Alessio's youngest brother, Guido, a grumpy fifteen-year-old. They'd made excellent company for each other: the morose teenager who wanted to be roaming the streets with his mates and the disgruntled thirty-four-year-old man who wanted to be getting naked with his Irish fox.

When the hour had passed he'd gone up to the room and, the moment he'd crossed the threshold, she'd hurried out of the bathroom, hair straighteners in hand and only a towel wrapped around her.

'If you touch me, I swear I'll kick your ankles.' And then she'd hurried back in and locked the door.

Thirty minutes later she had opened the door a crack. 'Get to the other side of the room,' she'd ordered, and waited until he'd complied before stepping out.

She'd held her palms out in a warning. 'I mean it, Moncada. Don't touch me. It's taken me an hour to get my hair right.'

She was fully dressed, her hair loose and in sleek waves around her bare shoulders.

She'd been right to warn him to keep his distance.

If she'd been within arm's reach he would have had her in his hold quicker than she could blink. And they both knew what would have happened then.

He'd already ruined one of her outfits. The replacement dress for the evening reception was en route from Palermo. There was no time to get a replacement dress for the wedding itself.

He figured he had five, maybe six hours until he could make love to her again. There was a three-hour window between the wedding breakfast and the evening reception. That was plenty of time to make love again, maybe twice, and still have time to shower and change.

*Dio*, he was planning when he could make love to her again?

'Talk to me. Distract me,' he ordered.

'What? Why?'

'Because, *dolcezza*, me driving with a rock-hard erection is going to get us killed. I need a distraction. Tell me something interesting about European medieval history.'

She giggled softly. 'It's all interesting.'

'Narrow it down. Tell me something about Sicily I don't know.'

'Do you know much about how Sicily became a part of the Crown of Aragon?'

'When we were ruled by Spain?'

'That's the one.'

'Educate me.'

For the next ten minutes he relaxed and listened as she told him about a period in his island's history that was familiar to him only on a distant level, bringing it to life in that wonderful lyrical way she had.

'If you're set against being a teacher, have you thought of being a historian?' he asked. 'You could work in a museum giving tours and educating the public.'

'But that would take me away from home,' she pointed out. 'There are no museums near to where we live so to do that would mean having to move away from Orla and Finn.'

'I'm sure they would miss you but Orla will be able to afford professional help rather than rely on you.'

'I would miss them too much,' she stated simply.

'Then get them to move with you. It's time you started living your life for yourself. You've put it on hold for long enough.'

Parking at the cathedral was limited but he found a space easily enough. As he held Aislin's hand to help her out, a figure in the distance caught his attention.

He swore.

Aislin followed his gaze and saw a couple heading their way. The elderly man had a walking stick and a shock of pure white hair that brought to mind Albert Einstein. The much younger, pencil-thin woman holding his arm had dark hair coiffured within an inch of its life and wore a chic silver lace dress and billowing green silk cape. She guessed they were grandfather and granddaughter.

Then she looked back at Dante and saw the distaste curdling his face and felt suddenly sure it was because of the woman he was staring at.

Nausea sparked in her guts, violent and immediate.

Katrina might not be one of his ex-lovers but the odds were that another guest or two would be.

'Who's that?' she asked as casually as she could manage.

'My mother.'

*'What?'*

'That woman is my mother.'

*That* woman spotted them staring and raised a hand in their direction to wave enthusiastically.

Dante raised a hand in return. He didn't wave it.

'That's your mother? You're kidding me! Seriously?' Aislin, all nausea gone as quickly as it had come, now had the worry that her eyes were going to pop out. Holy moly, that was his *mother*?

She didn't look like any mother of a thirty-four-year-old man Aislin had ever met.

'She could be your sister.'

'Be sure to tell her that. She might love you as much as she loves her plastic surgeon.'

'He must be a very expensive plastic surgeon. Her face is amazing.' Aislin lowered her voice as the couple inched closer to them, their speed hindered by the man's struggle to walk. 'And is that your grandfather?'

'That man, I am guessing, is her latest future ex-husband.'

About to snigger, she noticed Dante's face had become blank.

The snigger died on her lips.

In all their many conversations, Dante had said little about his mother other than that she'd moved to the Italian mainland when Dante had been small… without her only child.

She slipped her hand into his, suddenly feeling protective of him.

As Immacolata came into clearer vision, walking effortlessly on heels that had to be twice the three inches Aislin had braved, her curiosity intensified.

Probably around the same height as Aislin without the heels, that was the only similarity between the two women. Immacolata was as dark as her son, although Aislin would bet the colouring now came from a bottle. Up close, she looked older than first impressions, but still nowhere near old enough to have an adult child. Elegant and beautiful, her startling blue eyes were bright with mischief.

'Dante!' she cried, releasing her partner's arm to embrace her son and kiss his cheeks.

'Mother,' Dante replied returning her greeting coolly. 'Are you going to introduce us?'

'Dante, this is Giuseppe, a good friend of Riccardo D'Amore and a very dear friend of mine. His wife has recently departed, rest her soul.' She made the sign of the cross in a tremendous show of piety. 'Giuseppe, this is Dante.'

He didn't think his mother had acknowledged him as her son since he'd turned eighteen. It would have made people question her own age too closely.

Giuseppe bowed his head and accepted Dante's dutiful embrace. He was so ancient a gust of wind could have knocked him off his feet.

'Helping him get over her death, are you?' he asked his mother in an undertone.

'I do my best,' she said with a demureness that would have made him laugh if it had come from anyone but the woman who had carried and given birth to him. 'He's almost worth as much as you are, darling.'

'Where's Pierre?' Pierre was husband number five.

'Pierre's history.'

'What did he do?'

'Bored me.' She winked at Aislin, who was watching their exchange with a furrowed brow, and then said, 'Who is this beauty?'

'This is Aislin,' he replied, then switched to English. 'Aislin, this is my *mother*, Immacolata.'

His mother gave the slightest of winces as he stressed her relationship to him. She didn't speak English but some words translated into every language.

It gave him a perverse if fleeting dose of satisfaction.

Aislin allowed herself to be enveloped in his mother's cloud of perfume and said, 'It's wonderful to meet you.'

His mother smiled, not understanding a word she'd said. However, she noticed Aislin's hand and grabbed it, examining the ring on her finger.

Then she turned accusing eyes to Dante. 'Did you give her this ring?'

'Yes.'

'You're getting married? You didn't tell me.'

'One, it is a very recent engagement, and two, you didn't bother to tell me you were marrying Pierre or Stavros until after you'd married them.'

As the crowd by the cathedral was growing, Dante thought it past time to cut the conversation short and reclaimed Aislin's hand to join the congregation.

Once they were seated and waiting for the bride to make her grand entrance, both of them making a beeline for the back of the cathedral, Aislin immediately whispered, 'What did I miss?'

He filled her in briefly.

'So she's dumped your stepdad for a richer widower?' she summarised.

'They don't call her the Black Widow for nothing,'

he said shortly. 'Pierre is her fifth husband and about to become considerably poorer, like all the husbands before him, my father included.'

The orchestra began to play the tune to mark the bride's arrival and the congregation rose to its feet.

After Cristina had made the long walk down the aisle and they'd sat back down for the priest to begin his sermon, Aislin asked quietly, 'How old were you when your mother left?' The woman on her other side was dealing with a fractious baby, its noise enough to cover any illicit conversation.

'Seven.'

'Did she leave because she found out about my mother being pregnant by your father?'

'I don't know why she left.'

Her heart clenched for the abandoned boy. 'Have you never asked?'

'No. She left. End of story.'

'Do I have to worry about her scratching my eyes out when she discovers who I am? And she *will* discover it. Someone is bound to tell her.'

'She's more likely to be curious about you.' He closed his eyes and took a long inhale. 'To be fair to my mother, she's not a cruel woman. She wouldn't blame you for your mother's sin.'

'*My* mother's sin?' Her eyes turned to lasers. 'My mother was nineteen when your father seduced her.'

He sighed. 'I didn't mean to put the finger of blame on her. I didn't know she was that young.'

She was silent for a moment. 'To be fair to your father, from what our mother told us, she knew he was married.'

He asked one of the many questions he'd been denying to himself that he was curious about. 'Do you know how they met?'

'She was on holiday with some girlfriends here in Sicily. Your father knew the owner of their hotel. He saw my mum sunbathing by the pool and it was lust at first sight.' Her eyes hardened. 'It was supposed to be a holiday romance but they were careless. They agreed she would raise Orla and his only contribution would be financial. It suited them both. Poor Orla, she wanted so badly to know him, but was never allowed.'

The priest finished his sermon and invited the congregation to their feet to sing a hymn. The words were in Latin but Aislin knew the tune and happily joined in.

Mass had been a huge part of her childhood and this ceremony, although conducted in a different language, had the same feel to it.

Four rows in front of them, she could see Immacolata Whatever-Her-Surname-Currently-Was belting the hymn out with the best of them.

'Did you see much of your mother after she left?' she asked when they were again invited to sit back down.

'Some. She moved to Florence. I would stay with her for weekends and some holidays.'

Aislin thought of her father. Their relationship had been similar but she had no memory of living with him so had never missed him as a permanent presence. 'You must have missed her.'

He shrugged. 'I would have missed my father more if he'd left.'

'I'm sorry.' She squeezed his fingers, thinking how hard it must be for him. Here she was rabbiting on about their families and the past when he was still dealing with his grief at losing his father and coping with the secrets and lies that had been revealed. 'Do you think she knew that you would miss your father more and that's why she left you with him?'

'I think she was thinking only of herself. Mothers are supposed to nurture. Mine is only interested in nurturing her fingernails. It goes against her grain. It always did.'

She gave him a rueful smile. 'My mother's not really the nurturing type either, in case you hadn't realised.'

No, Dante thought. Aislin was the nurturer in the O'Reilly family.

Little wonder she was so fiercely protective of her sister and nephew. For Aislin, her little family meant everything.

A memory came to him, one he hadn't thought of in a long time, from when a decade ago he'd suffered a nasty bout of flu. For two weeks he'd hardly been able to lift his head up. When his mother had learned of this she had come swanning in to check up on him. She'd stood at the threshold of his bedroom door with a mask covering her fully made-up face and even in his weakened state he'd been disdainful at the distance she'd kept.

For the first time he appreciated that she'd made the effort to see him and satisfy herself that he wasn't about to die. She'd stayed in his home, uninvited, for five days, never getting any closer to him than the bedroom door, but she had stayed until he was over the worst of it and then flown back to whichever husband she'd been married to.

In her own way she did care for him.

If he were in an accident that left him in a coma he was quite sure she would be at his bedside—no germs to worry about from a car accident—and that she would stay until the danger had passed.

When his father had suffered his fatal heart attack she'd flown straight over to be with Dante.

*Had* she known about Orla? Had she conspired with his father to keep it secret from him?

The pounding increased, the familiar churning in his guts swirling with the poison of all the secrets and lies.

The congregation rose, again, to its feet. Another hymn was sung and then it was time for the exchange of vows.

The noises in his head were loud enough to block their words out and he was glad of it. Love and fidelity were empty promises. Tying yourself into a union where the only guarantee was disappointment, because that was what family amounted to. Disappointment.

Aislin's view of the bride and groom was restricted but Alessio's and Cristina's unwavering voices rang clear and true through the great walls of the cathedral. The solemnity of the occasion suddenly clutched at her and she felt something move and shift within her. The lump she'd found in her throat that morning when she'd watched Dante sleeping came back and she became aware all over again of his fingers clasped through hers.

A week ago, she would have laughed if anyone had suggested she would feel so moved to witness a couple pledge their lives to each other, but there was something so affirming about the moment, the faith

Alessio and Cristina had in each other and the love they shared, that Aislin had to keep her face forward, suddenly afraid to look at Dante.

Would she one day be told by Orla that Dante had surprised even himself by falling in love with someone and that he was going to be married for real?

The slice to her heart at this thought almost made her gasp from the pain.

It took a few moments for her to loosen her grip on Dante's hand.

She was just being sentimental. Weddings did that to people. It was natural to be caught up in the romance and joy of these occasions. When a new day started the feelings would be nothing but a memory.

In two days, Dante would be nothing but a memory too, albeit a memory that was going to be on the fringe of her life for the rest of her existence.

'Do you think they'll last?' she asked him as they filed out with the rest of the congregation to the cathedral grounds for the photographs.

He nodded. 'They both come from families where marriage is sacrosanct. Even if they make each other miserable they'll stay together.'

'Not all marriages end in misery,' she said wistfully.

'No, they all end in death or divorce.'

And then their conversation was cut off as the photographer took control and began ordering everyone into position.

Aislin fixed a smile to her face and joined the heaving crowd.

The happy couple were photographed on their own first, then immediate family were brought in, then extended family. Finally she and Dante were called in with the other friends to take their position.

Dante placed his arm around her waist and held her close and, as they all smiled for the camera, all she could think was that this picture would be the only physical evidence left of her time with him.

# CHAPTER THIRTEEN

'CAN YOU DO the buttons up for me, please?'

Dante, who'd been trimming his beard, left the bathroom and stood behind her.

Aislin's face when they'd walked into their room and she'd seen the replacement dress hanging on the wardrobe had been a picture in itself.

She'd put her forefinger and thumb together. 'I came this close to choosing this dress.'

'So I heard. What stopped you?'

'I thought I would look a fool in it.'

'You could never look a fool.' And then, because it had been a good six hours since he'd last made love to her, he'd taken her to bed.

Losing himself in her eager, welcoming body had been enough to dislodge the bitterness the wedding had brought out in him.

He felt himself stiffen to remember all the things they had done to each other.

Catching his eye in the reflection of the mirror they were stood in front of, Aislin gave him her best school-teacher look. 'Just the buttons, Moncada.'

He saluted then set to work on the tiny gold buttons that would keep the dress in place.

Done, he stayed where he was, content to gaze at her. 'You're beautiful.'

Her cheeks pinked and she smiled. 'So are you.'

'I'm glad we ruined your first dress.'

'So am I.'

The replacement dress was strapless and skimmed the top of her cleavage. Dark cream with embellished gold embroidery, it hugged her waist and flared at her hips, falling to her calves at the front and to her ankles at the back. The personal shopper had matched it with cream high heels.

As their love-making had ruined her hair again, she'd twisted it into another knot. Like the night before, the knot was messy but striking, and suited her perfectly. Like the night before, he wouldn't have her any other way. He liked that she'd never been one to perfect hairdos over and over until she could create them with her eyes closed.

'We should go before I give in to temptation and ruin this dress too.'

She hooked her arms around his neck and pressed her lips lightly to his. 'When we get back to the room later, I will help you ruin it.'

He groaned and forced his legs back, away from her.

Feeling giddy and full of fizz, as if she could jump up and defy gravity to fly, Aislin held his hand tightly to keep her grounded on their walk to the ballroom, where the evening reception party was being held.

She would not allow herself to think that this was their last night together or dissect why his cynical comments about marriage had struck like a blow.

This was a night for celebration and their last opportunity to convince Riccardo D'Amore that they were in love.

She would not allow herself to acknowledge the wrench in her heart or what it meant.

As they walked through the banquet room, tonight transformed into a second bar, a man striding towards them caught her eye and stopped her in her tracks. As tall as Dante and almost as handsome, there was something about him…

'Who's that?' The whispered question was hardly out of her mouth when the man spotted Dante.

He greeted him with a huge embrace and kisses to his cheeks. They exchanged a few words before he waved an apologetic hand and hurried off.

'Who was that?' she repeated.

Dante stared at her with narrowed eyes. 'Tonino Valente. Why do you ask?'

'There's something familiar about him.' She screwed up her eyes, trying to think where she'd seen him before.

'He owns the castle. Riccardo is throwing his weight around and keeping all the staff on their toes. Tonino's flown in to troubleshoot.'

'How do you know him?'

'His father and my father were friends. His father owned a hotel chain… I would not be surprised if it was one of his hotels that your mother stayed at when she met my father.'

And just like that it came to her why he looked so familiar and she clamped a hand over her mouth.

'What's wrong?' he asked.

She swallowed and, without thinking, said, 'He reminds me of Finn.'

'Orla's son?'

She nodded. 'Orla came to Sicily six months before her accident. She wanted to meet your father but lost her nerve. That's all she told me about her time here but a month later she discovered she was pregnant. She always refused to say who the father was and I assumed it was a work colleague or something. She always promised she would tell him after the birth… Oh, how could I have been so blind? The dates fit!'

And then, suddenly realising who she was spilling her spiralling thoughts to, grabbed Dante's hand and pressed it to her chest to stare at him earnestly. 'You can't say anything. I might be completely wrong—I probably *am* completely wrong—so promise me you'll keep your mouth shut. Orla would *kill* me if she knew I'd been speculating like this.'

He didn't say anything.

'*Please*, Dante,' she begged. 'Don't say anything to Orla. Or to Tonino. My imagination's just gone a little haywire, that's all. I should have kept my thoughts to myself.'

Yes, she should have, Dante thought grimly. If she didn't learn to control them better, then one day Aislin's overactive imagination and unfiltered mouth would get her into trouble. The thought of Tonino Valente being Finn's father was ludicrous.

But her wild speculation wasn't the cause of the needles driving through his skin.

He'd seen the way she'd looked at Tonino and then, when she had asked about him, he'd experienced something hot and rancid in his guts he had never felt before.

It had been a feeling he suspected felt much like jealousy would feel.

Dante had never been jealous of anyone or anything in his life.

But what else accounted for the burst of relief when she'd explained why Tonino had caught her attention?

He stared at Aislin with the feeling of a man standing in quicksand.

Barely a week with her, only a couple of days as lovers, and he'd had a moment where he had wanted to rip the head off an old friend's neck.

Her eyes were pleading with him. 'Please, Dante, promise you won't say anything.'

As he had no intention of meeting Orla, it was the easiest promise he would ever make. The stab of guilt he felt when making it was as ludicrous as Aislin's speculation.

He had made no promises about meeting his father's secret love-child or her son. He'd been non-committal at best regarding the invitation to Finn's party, and after this day and the virulent feelings that had almost choked him at seeing his mother, the lies and deceptions of his life brought back to the forefront where his time with Aislin had calmed them, he was relieved he'd made no specific promises.

Dante never wanted to be part of a family unit again and that included one with his secret sister who, he knew, was as great a liar as their father.

He rationalised that all these heated, irrational, jealous feelings and all the needles digging into him had been dredged up by what Aislin represented: their shared sister and his father's lies.

They were nothing to do with Aislin herself. He

liked her company. His struggle to keep his hands off her was due to their time together coming with a predetermined limit heightening the effect.

And, as he thought all this, a modicum of calm settled back into him.

This was a heightened situation. That was all.

He would enjoy the time he had left with Aislin and then say goodbye to her without a second thought.

As great as she was, she was everything he didn't want. This was a woman who had put her life on hold for three years to nurture and care for her sister and nephew during a period in which she should have been making the most of her youth and freedom. She'd done it because she loved them. For Aislin, family meant everything, where for him, family meant nothing.

His feelings for her were nothing extraordinary.

Aislin pushed all thoughts about Tonino Valente away, recognising that her imagination had briefly got the better of her, and instead concentrated on the wedding reception.

She'd been to many weddings in her life but this one topped the lot. The ballroom had been transformed into a sparkly wonderland complete with a champagne fountain that had to break all world records, a chocolate fountain that no one above the age of ten could get near, a cocktail bar, an ever-replenished array of canapés served by an army of waiting staff…all of it set to music pumping out courtesy of a world-famous DJ who had recently hit number one in every continent with his remix of a classic eighties tune.

The atmosphere was pumping as much as the music and she had a whale of a time, drinking lager from a bottle—Dante assured her that propriety should be damned—and chatting to Sabine and her husband, Francois, who after a few drinks loosened up and became excellent company too. Other guests joined them, dipping in and out of the conversation.

All Aislin's feelings of inadequacy had gone. Not even Katrina's malicious presence bothered her. She felt nothing but pity for the beautiful woman trapped in a hell of her own making.

The only fly in the ointment was Dante.

Something was bugging him, she was certain of it. It was nothing she could put her finger on, as outwardly he was his usual sociable self, but she detected an undercurrent to his mood.

Aislin was catching her breath at their table after a vigorous dance with Sabine when Riccardo D'Amore came over to them.

'You drink beer?' he asked her, his brow creased.

She nodded cheerfully. 'Champagne gives me a headache.'

'No cocktail?'

'Not tonight. Too many and I'll get drunk, and then I'll probably fall over and make a fool of myself, so it's safer for me to stick to beer.'

Dante doubted Riccardo had understood half of what she'd just told him in that rapid-fire delivery, but he beamed nonetheless.

And then he turned to Dante. 'Are you free Monday morning?' he asked in their own language.

'That depends why you're asking.'

'I've been having a rethink about that deal you made with Alessio. I think I was a little hasty in my involvement. Alessio has a good head on his shoulders.'

That was as close to an apology as Dante would get but he didn't expect a full one. Riccardo was a proud man. He did not like to admit his mistakes.

'What are you saying?' He wanted it spelt out.

'That I was wrong to interfere. I have spoken to him and he is still of the opinion that the deal with you is the best one on the table. The contracts are still drawn up. He goes on his honeymoon Monday afternoon but can spare a few minutes to sign it before he leaves. That is, if the deal is something you still wish to go ahead with?'

Hiding his euphoria at his plan succeeding so perfectly, Dante pretended to consider the question. 'I have meetings all day Monday. My lawyer will be with me. If Alessio can bring the contract and his lawyers to me for eleven a.m., I should have a window to fit him in then.'

Dante had his pride too. He wanted this deal—he wouldn't have offered Aislin such a large amount of money if it wasn't so important to him—but he would not roll over and demean himself by snatching Riccardo's olive branch without making the man sweat a little. It was the least he deserved. Alessio too, for allowing his father to browbeat him into pulling out of the deal in the first place.

'You are still willing to go ahead?'

'If he can get to me for eleven, then yes.'

'He will be there. Where will you be?'

'Madrid. I fly there tomorrow evening.' His tone left no doubt—Riccardo and Alessio could take it or leave it.

Riccardo pulled his handkerchief out of his top

pocket and patted his perspiring forehead. 'He will be there.'

Dante finally allowed himself a smile and extended his hand. 'Then we have a deal.'

Riccardo clasped it in his clammy paw. 'We have a deal.'

When Aislin opened her eyes the next morning there was a cramping weight in her chest so heavy that it took a few moments before she could breathe with any ease. Dante's arm was draped over her belly, his knee nudging against her thigh, sleeping deeply.

His mood had much improved once the deal with the D'Amores was confirmed as back on. He'd joined her on the packed dance floor and neither had complained that the mass of bodies forced them to hold each other closely.

The euphoric mood had extended to the bedroom. Little in the way of sleep had been found in their bed that night, even less than the night before.

Aislin hadn't wanted to fall sleep. She hadn't wanted to miss a single moment.

But nature had taken its course and she'd been pulled into slumber as the first glimpse of sunlight broke through the join in the heavy curtains.

Hot tears bit into her retinas and she blinked vigorously to contain them.

Her chest *hurt*. Her stomach hurt too, filled with knots being pulled into a giant tangle of pain.

Dante shifted closer and stretched. His arousal replaced his knee against her thigh.

She mustn't cry.

They still had a few hours left.

And maybe…

He slid on top of her and covered her mouth with his.

Maybe Dante wasn't ready to say goodbye yet either.

Breakfast was served in the dining room. The guests who had spent the weekend celebrating with the happy couple were all accounted for, present in body if not in spirit. An awful lot of heads were being clutched and painkillers being swapped like sweets. Only the children had retained their manic spirits but, where they had spent the weekend being indulged, this morning they were shushed.

Aislin couldn't work out why she felt so bad, considering she'd paced her alcohol intake and made sure to drink plenty of water.

Dante didn't look much better either but insisted with a brisk smile that he felt fine. His appetite was as healthy as always.

Although she had little appetite of her own, Aislin took her time, picking at the croissants, chewing slowly, refilling her coffee and orange juice numerous times; anything to drag this last meal out.

Yet, though she tried her hardest to make the time pass as slowly as was humanly possible, she found it hard to look at him. Every time she met his eyes her heart would swell and she would find herself biting her tongue from the plea it longed to shoot out.

*Is this really it?*

Was it really possible that in the space of a week she had gone from thinking she would never get involved with another man, especially not this one, to feeling her insides would rip to shreds if she never felt his arms around her again?

He was nothing like the man she had imagined.

Just as Dante pushed his chair back, ready to leave the dining room, Riccardo D'Amore and his wife stopped at their table.

'Good morning,' he said in English, smiling, no sign of a headache or any ill-effects from the night before.

'Morning,' Aislin replied as cheerfully as she could manage.

'We like you to come to house for dinner.' He spoke carefully.

'Me and Dante?' She did her best to hide her surprise.

'*Sì*. It will be great pleasure for us. You come… *mercoledì*?'

She glanced at Dante. His lips were curved upwards but the expression in his eyes gave nothing away.

'Mercoledi?' she repeated uncertainly.

'Wednesday,' Dante murmured.

'Right. Wednesday.' Her heart made a sudden leap. She could stay until Wednesday. That was totally doable. Orla could cope a few more days without her and Aislin could have an extra four days with Dante!

Feeling a whole heap lighter inside, she grinned with the whole of her face. 'I don't have anything planned for Wednesday. Have you anything in your diary?' she directed at Dante.

He shook his head.

'It's a date.'

Riccardo translated for his wife, who showed her pleasure by beaming as widely as her husband.

Back in their room, Aislin began to pack her things in her super-posh suitcase, practically dancing a jig with happiness.

Four more nights with Dante! Perfect. She'd give Orla a call in a few minutes and let her know…

'Do you want the balance of the money transferred to Orla?' Dante asked, breaking through her happy thoughts.

'Yes, please.' She bounded over to him and threw her arms around his neck. 'You must be delighted your plan has worked out so well.'

Expecting a kiss, she was disappointed when he kept his gaze focused over the top of her head. 'It is good that he saw reason. The deal with me will make the D'Amores far more money than the deal with my competitor would have.'

'Well, I for one am thrilled it's all worked out for you.'

He gave a tight smile and unhooked her arms from his neck. 'I'll transfer the money now.' He stepped away and removed his phone from his jacket pocket.

'I'll call Orla and let her know to expect it, and let her know I won't be back until Thursday.'

'Thursday?'

'The D'Amore dinner's on Wednesday,' she reminded him.

He perched on the armchair and gave his attention to his phone. 'There will not be a dinner.'

Her stomach dropped like a brick. 'But we said we were going.'

He raised a hefty shoulder nonchalantly.

'Surely you don't want to upset him this late in the day?'

He shrugged again. His fingers were busy working on his phone. 'The contract will be signed tomorrow.'

'Is there not a grace period for him to change his mind?'

'No. Once it is signed, then that's it.'

'So you lied about going to his house for dinner?'

'You agreed to it, not me.'

She stared at him, willing him to look up from his phone so she could see what was in his eyes.

'You said you were free,' she pointed out evenly. The crushing weight was expanding but she refused to acknowledge it. Her overactive imagination could be leading her on a path that was something out of nothing. Dante had made no secret to her of his dislike for Riccardo and, after the way Riccardo had treated him, she understood why he would be reluctant to accept his hospitality.

He probably thought, too, that he would be putting her out. After all, she had told him only the day before that she could never move from her home because she would miss Orla and Finn too much.

He was being considerate.

'It is not important,' he said. 'I will let him know after the contract is signed that we won't be attending.'

'I don't mind going. You're going to have to work with him…'

'No, I will be working with his son.'

'But his feelings will be hurt.'

'I will let him down gently. It was not my company they desired but yours.'

'Honestly, Dante, I don't mind staying a few extra days. It's the least I can do for you.'

He grimaced. 'I'm flying to Madrid tonight and have back-to-back meetings for the next two days.'

'I've never been to Madrid.'

'It's a beautiful city and I recommend you visit it one day.'

One day?

'Dante... Don't you like the idea of us having a few more days together?'

'It would be fun if I had the time, but I don't.'

Fun?

'Have I done something to upset you?'

'No. You've played your part very well... *Va bene.*' His tone lifted a notch. 'The money has been transferred. I will charter a flight back to Ireland for you this afternoon. I would lend you my jet but I need it to get to Madrid. I'll have a car waiting at the airport to drive you home.' He finally looked up from his phone.

The blankness in the eyes, normally so full of expression and life, was enough to make her blood freeze.

'Have you finished packing? We need to go.'

# CHAPTER FOURTEEN

DANTE DROVE THE car out of the castle grounds and took the route straight to the airport.

He would drop Aislin there then go home and get himself organised for his flight to Madrid.

He stretched his mind to the coming week and the business he needed to take care of. Now that the deal with the D'Amores was back on, he would need to reschedule appointments and get systems up and running. There was a lot of work in the weeks and months ahead.

Aislin's phone rang, cutting through the silence.

They hadn't exchanged a word since getting into his car.

She'd been her usual bright, bubbly self when saying goodbye to everyone but he had sensed the melancholy beneath it and had the strangest feeling he had hurt her.

It had been good of her to offer to stay with him and attend the dinner with Riccardo but he had put her out enough.

It was time to say goodbye. Their job was done.

There was no reason for him to prolong their time together, something he had told himself with resolute firmness when he had showered that morning before breakfast.

He'd enjoyed some great times with her, but now it was over, exactly as had been agreed right at the very start of it all. His feelings on the matter had only hardened.

'Are you not going to answer that?' he asked when she ignored her phone.

'It'll be Orla.'

'Then why not answer it?'

'Because I know what she's going to ask and I don't have an answer for her.'

'What do you think she wants?'

'I know what she wants. She wants to know if she can meet you before Finn's party.'

His hands tightened on the steering wheel but his heart lifted to see the airport on the horizon.

He put his foot on the accelerator.

Almost there.

A few more minutes and she would be out of his car and out of his life for good, and he would never have to think about the O'Reillys again.

'Fine,' she said through what sounded like gritted teeth.

Nothing more was said until he pulled into the airport's drop-off.

He switched the engine off, twisted in his seat to face her and found himself looking at the back of her head.

'There is a member of the airport staff in the departure lounge waiting for you,' he said. 'She'll have your name on a board, so you can't miss her. She will see you're looked after and get you where you need to go.'

She didn't answer.

'Aislin?'

Her head moved round slowly and then the grey eyes he'd found so striking in that very first glance fixed on him, and what he saw in them was powerful enough to make his heart thump and twist.

Then she blinked and the hurt he'd seen was gone.

'Get your phone out,' she said briskly. 'I'll give you Orla's number and you can call her when the DNA test's done.'

Blood surged in his head. 'Aislin—'

'Will you give me your number too, so I can pass it on to her?' she continued, as if he hadn't tried to speak. 'Even if you don't want to meet before the party it would be good for the two of you to talk.'

He took a deep breath and rested his pounding head back. 'No.'

'No…? What do you mean?'

He'd hoped she would leave without the need for this conversation but she had boxed him in. Non-committal answers were not going to satisfy her now. 'I'm not going to meet Orla.'

'Not meet her…?' She looked as confused as if he'd told her the sky was really a giant mushroom. 'But why would you not want to meet her? She's your sister. Sure, she can be annoying, but she's a lovely person—'

'Orla is not my sister.' Something crawled inside him. It twisted in his veins and bound to his bones, pulsing rabidly under his skin.

'Not this again. She *is* your sister.'

'No, *dolcezza*, she is not.' It was a fight to keep his tone even. 'The test will prove she shares my DNA but that does not make her my sister. I understand that this is not what you have hoped for, but she is a stranger to me, and I have no wish to allow a stranger into my life.'

'You'll have to meet her at Finn's party. You won't be able to avoid her there.'

'I'm not coming to Finn's party.'

'But you said…'

'I said to give me the details. I made no promises.'

'Dante, *please* come. Give them a chance…'

*'No!'*

Suddenly furious at her refusal to listen, furious at the emotions she dredged up in him, furious that even now when they were saying goodbye there was an ache deep inside him to haul her into his arms, even furious at the shocked widening of her eyes, he slammed his hands on the steering wheel.

Everything he'd been suppressing in the hope of being rid of her without a scene spilled out like venom.

'This is not about chances. I do not want them in my life. I am *sick* of family and all the lies and deceptions that come with them. Sick of it. What does Orla want from me? My money? She has a million euros of it. She has lived her life for twenty-seven years without me, why want me now? My father… Damn him to hell!'

With a roar that erupted from nowhere, he punched the wheel hard enough to bruise. 'All my adult life I have bailed him out. I kept a roof over his head when he blew everything my grandparents and their parents before them built. I helped him whenever he needed me. I loved him, and all that's left is this monstrous lie, and don't let me start talking about my self-obsessed mother, who bores of everything and everyone, even her own child.

'I look at my extended family and see nothing but misery; siblings hating and bitching about siblings, spouses cheating, hypocritical parents moralising, all pretending that their lives are great, when underneath it's all rotten. I don't want any of it. I am not a gambling man but, even if I were, I know the odds would not be in my favour of anything good coming from a sister who I already know is a liar like our father. Whoever the father of her child is, he has a right to know, but she keeps it a secret from him when she knows the damage such secrets cause.'

Aislin had shrunk back during his diatribe, but now she leaned forward, bright red colour slashing her cheeks. 'If you knew Orla you would know she would only keep such a thing secret for good reason.'

'I have only your word for that.'

'Is my word not good enough? Hasn't the time we've spent together this past week proven that I'm a woman of my word?'

'I take no one at their word,' he bit back.

'And I thought *I* was distrustful…' Aislin shook her head and tried to control the tempest raging within her.

Bad enough he should be so cynical about Orla but to be so cynical about *her*, after everything they had shared… That hurt more than she had dreamed possible, more than his offhand refusal that she stay the extra days as she had offered.

He'd had his fun with her and, now their time was up, he was happy to discard her as if nothing had happened.

'You know, sir, you're not the only one who has

been hurt and let down—it happens to everyone. My mother left the country when I was nineteen and I don't think she's ever coming back. She left me to deal with the fallout after Orla's accident—and, while we're talking about Orla, need I remind you that she is the one who has spent her life with a father who is only a name and a mother who couldn't be bothered to visit her when she was close to death or meet her seriously ill grandson? You don't see Orla feeling sorry for herself.'

Warming to her theme, she straightened her shoulders. 'My good-for-nothing ex cheated on me when my sister and nephew were hovering between life and death in that godforsaken hospital. I honestly thought I would never trust anyone apart from my sister again. I came this close…' she put her thumb and forefinger together, right in his stony face '…to trusting you. I thought you were an exaggerated version of him but then I got to know you and I *stupidly* allowed myself to believe you were one of the good guys, but you're not. You're worse. You let me believe you would come to Finn's party…'

'You let yourself believe that.'

'Stop with the lies and excuses!' The angst and panic that had been clawing at her suddenly exploded. 'You're nothing but a liar and I cannot believe I was so blind and so *stupid*!' She slammed her clenched fists onto her lap in her rage. 'Orla and Finn think you're going to be a part of their lives. You're the one who gave me the false hope to let them believe that. You've made a liar of me, and now I'm going to have to hurt them with the truth when I would rather cut a limb off than see them hurt.

'You've tricked Riccardo into believing you're now all family orientated, when you'd rather puke on your own shoes than have a family, and you have the nerve to call *Orla* a liar? You're the biggest liar of all. You're just another selfish bastard but you have the money to throw at your problems and make them go away. Ooh, I need to fake an engagement…let's pay someone. Ooh, a sister I've never met…have some money. Ooh, a seriously ill nephew…have some money. Job done, because obviously that's all they would ever want from you, and it's a good thing that's all you have to offer because you're not fit to lick my sister's boots.'

A sharp rapping on the window brought them both up short.

Dante punched the button to open the window and a uniformed attendant immediately stuck his head in, blabbering rapidly. Aislin didn't need to speak the language to know they were being told to move.

'Don't worry, I'm going.' She pulled the engagement ring from her finger and threw it on the car floor, unwilling to look at his lying face one more time. 'Have a nice life, *sir*.'

Then she grabbed her handbag, jumped out of the car and slammed the door shut behind her.

The roar of his engine and squealing tyres rang in her ears as she walked into the departure gate.

Only when the member of staff who held Aislin's name on a board asked where her luggage was did she remember she'd left it in the boot of Dante's car.

The chartered plane hurtled down the runway and lifted into the air.

Aislin kept her gaze fixed on the English magazine she'd brought. She would not watch Sicily disappear from view.

She would not think of the man she was leaving behind.

She would never think of him again.

In a few hours she would be back with the two people she loved the most in the world.

She would pick her life up where she'd left it but now she would allow herself to think of her own needs too.

She would make something of her life.

And she would never think of Sicily again.

Dante's mother was already seated in a corner of the restaurant when he entered it, a large glass of white wine in her hand. She rose to her feet with a big smile and embraced him tightly.

'This is an unexpected pleasure,' she said, sitting back down. 'Is your Irish beauty not joining us?'

He took his own seat with a grimace. 'Aislin's in Ireland.'

His mother looked at him shrewdly. 'Trouble in paradise?'

'It's over,' he said shortly, then attempted a smile. 'Have you looked at the menu?'

A waiter came over to take their order. As soon as he left them, Dante's mother leaned forward. 'What happened?'

He feigned bored ignorance. 'With what?'

'Your Irish beauty.'

'Nothing happened. We just decided marriage was a step too far.'

She cast him that shrewd look again. 'That's a shame. I liked her. You liked her too.'

'Mother…' he said warningly. He'd never discussed his love life with her before and was not about to start now.

The last person he wanted to talk about was Aislin. All he had to do was recall their last conversation and his blood pressure would rise to dangerous levels.

'Okay, so you don't want to talk about her. What do you want to talk about? I assume there has to be a reason you've invited me here—you've never invited me to dinner before.'

He looked at her, feeling strangely discomfited. He'd picked up the tab on every occasion they'd dined out since he'd turned twenty.

Had none of those occasions come from his instigation? 'Haven't I?'

She waved a dismissive hand. 'It doesn't matter. What's on your mind? Or shall I make an educated guess and ask if it's about your sister?'

The nausea that curdled in his guts at this comment was almost as violent as the nausea he'd experienced when she'd mentioned Aislin.

He inhaled slowly then exhaled for even longer.

In the eight days that had passed since Aislin had slammed his car door, he'd failed to find the focus on work he needed. Instead he'd replayed their many conversations, especially those about his father, over and over, a loop playing so frequently he'd feared his head would combust.

He couldn't go on like this. He needed answers and his mother was the only person who could supply them.

'Is she the reason you left my father?'

Her perceptive eyes narrowed a touch then she gave

a sharp nod. 'I left him when I learned he'd got another woman pregnant but she wasn't the reason. I'd wanted to leave him for years—that affair was the excuse I'd been waiting for.'

Dante's glass of wine was brought to the table, along with a basket of freshly baked rolls.

He took a long drink. 'Why did you need an excuse?'

'To justify it to myself. The Irish woman wasn't the first woman he'd cheated on me with. She was just the first with real consequences.'

He took another sip of his wine then asked the question that had plagued him since Aislin had first suggested it might be for different reasons to what he'd always thought. 'Why didn't you take me?'

Her eyes softened. She rested her elbows on the table and folded her hands together under her chin. 'You were the reason I needed to find justification to leave. I knew I could never take you from him. Your father was a terrible husband but he was a wonderful father to you. And you adored him. When you fell over and hurt yourself, it was always him you would go to. When you had those nightmares when you were tiny, it was always him you called for. People thought I was a terrible mother for leaving you behind but I would have been a worse mother if I had taken you with me.'

Dante plucked a roll from the basket and pulled it apart with his fingers, taking a moment to gather his thoughts.

He *had* always instinctively gone to his father when he'd been in pain or fear. From as far back as he could remember he and his father had been as close as a father and son could be.

'Why didn't he tell me about Orla? Why didn't *you* tell me about her? Why all the secrecy?'

She sighed and reached for her wine. 'That was your father's choice and I had to respect his wishes. The mother didn't want him in the child's life. He could have fought for access but decided against it. He thought—and I agreed with him—that you had enough upheaval with me leaving without having to cope with the knowledge of a sister you would in all likelihood never meet. At the time it seemed the rational thing, the kind thing, to do.'

'Why did he never tell me when I was old enough to understand?'

'I don't know. I think, and of course this is only speculation, that he was afraid you would hate him for keeping it from you. You were the only person he ever truly loved. If it was not for you and having to raise you, I think his gambling problem would have got out of control a lot sooner than it did.'

Their first course was bought to them and then, for perhaps the first time in Dante's life, he and his mother really *talked*—about the past, his mother's life, her never-ending quest for a man who could make her happy.

He came to understand the choices she'd made, and that his father had made concerning him, had always been with the best of intentions. Hindsight might have proved those intentions to be faulty but they had done the best they could.

By the time they had finished their desserts and were sipping liqueur coffees he felt closer to her than he ever had before and it was with regret that he asked for the bill.

'Dante…' Tentatively, as if afraid he would shrug it off, she placed her hand on his. He let her. 'I know I have made many mistakes as your mother but can I give you the wisdom of my experience?'

Curious as to what she had to say, he nodded.

'I have married many times for many reasons and, yes, I admit financial security has always played a part in it, but I have always tried to love my husbands.'

He wanted to smile at her earnest way of admitting she was a gold-digger. His mother was nothing if not a character.

But he couldn't smile. All the muscles in his face had frozen.

Dread beat deep and heavy within him.

He knew where she was leading with this.

'Love is an elusive thing,' she said earnestly. 'It is very rare. When you find it, you have to grab hold of it and never let it go.' Her hold on his hand tightened as if to emphasise her point. 'Your Irish beauty… I don't know what has gone wrong between you, but when I watched you with her at the wedding I could feel the love you have for each other.'

'I am not in love with her.' His denial was automatic. He'd been denying it every one of the eight days since she had flown back to Ireland.

Just because he had fought his hands not to call her did not mean anything. Just because he had woken every day with an ache in his heart that he couldn't shift didn't mean anything either.

They had shared an intense few days together that had ended with bilious, hateful words. And then she had gone.

His mother tilted her head.

Was that *pity* he saw in her eyes?

'It was never love,' he said. 'It was a madness. That's all. It's over.'

She didn't say anything further on the subject but he could see exactly what she left unsaid.

That he was lying to himself.

## CHAPTER FIFTEEN

THE TINY END-OF-TERRACE house had a run-down feel to it but no sense of neglect. Even through the pouring Irish rain lashing his hire car, Dante could see the well-tended small front garden.

It had been five days since he'd dined with his mother and received the answers he'd sought. Five days of turmoil and dawning reason followed by self-recrimination and loathing.

He'd been a fool. He'd been everything Aislin had accused him of being.

Just the thought of her name made his heart twist.

As the days had passed, the hole that had lived inside him since she'd slammed his car door had widened.

What had started as a small fissure had become a gulf in his chest.

He'd thought speaking to his mother and making peace with his father would heal him, but how could he be healed when every time he closed his eyes Aislin's face appeared?

He had to see her.

Even if she slammed the door in his face, he could not leave things as they were. Their time together had been fleeting but had left its mark, had altered him in a fundamental way.

He could not live the rest of his life without seeing her face and hearing her Irish brogue.

Without getting to his knees and begging her forgiveness.

Without begging for another chance.

Without telling her that he loved her.

Because he did love her. Aislin brought sunshine wherever she went and the time they had spent together had infected him with its beaming radiance. She had switched a light on in him.

If he was condemned to spend the rest of his life without her sunshine, he wanted to be able to look at his reflection and say he had fought for her.

If she rejected him he would find a way to live with it. Whether she liked it or not, he was going to be part of her family now, because that was another gradual realisation his pig-headed brain had come to accept. He wanted to meet his sister and nephew. He wanted to be a part of their lives.

If Aislin loved them enough that she would lay her life down for them then that told him everything he needed to know about them.

A face appeared in the downstairs window.

Dante's heart slammed.

A moment later the front door opened.

A slim, pretty brunette appeared. She didn't move from the doorway, just stared at him.

On weighted legs, barely feeling the torrential rain falling on him, Dante made the short but excruciatingly long walk to his sister.

Staring into her green eyes was like looking in a mirror.

'I knew you'd come,' she said simply. Her voice was deeper than Aislin's but with the same brogue.

'How?' He hadn't known he was going to come until he'd woken that morning. It had been like waking from a long dream.

She smiled.

'Because you're my brother.'

And then she wrapped her arms around his rigid torso and held him so tightly that Dante found himself responding in kind, returning the embrace of this stranger who was not a stranger. His heart squeezed painfully, then expanded with a brand-new emotion filling it.

This was his sister. His *sister.* His blood.

They held each other for a long time before Orla kissed his cheek and led him into her home.

Finn, she told him as she made coffee in the tiniest kitchen Dante had ever been in, was sleeping. She would give him a little longer before waking him.

It was the opening he needed to ask, casually, where Aislin was.

'In Dublin. She's gone for a job interview.' A tinge of anxiety came into Orla's voice. 'But you'll see her next time… Will there be a next time?'

'Yes.' He took a deep breath. 'I'm sorry for letting you think any different. My head has not been in a good place. If the invitation is still open, I would very much like to come to Finn's party.'

'Of course the invitation's still open!' Her relief was instantaneous. 'I'm sure Aislin will be pleased to see you then too.'

The way Orla averted her eyes for the latter sent a weight plunging into his stomach. The look, coupled with her tone, told Dante clearly that he was the last person Aislin wanted to see.

'How is she?' As painful as the knowledge that Aislin despised him was, he needed to know she was okay.

'She's doing grand. Full of plans for the future. We're moving to Dublin—Aislin talked me into it. There's more resources there for Finn, and Aislin will have a better chance of finding a job she can use her degree for. I can never thank you enough for enabling this for us. You've changed our lives.'

Shortly afterwards, Orla carried Finn downstairs and sat him in his wheelchair. Only then did Dante truly understand the nature of his condition.

'Can he not walk?'

'He can but not for any length of time. His muscles are too weak. When we move to Dublin we'll have access to better treatment for him, so he has every chance of leading a near normal life.' Her brightness seemed forced, as if they were words Orla continually repeated to herself in the hope that repetition would make them come true.

He couldn't help himself from saying, 'Aislin helps you with him?'

Her eyes softened. 'If it wasn't for Aislin, neither of us would be here. I'm so happy she's finally getting her life back on track. She gave everything up for us and now it's my turn to support her.'

Many hours later it was with mixed emotions that Dante embraced his sister and nephew goodbye.

The blood bond between them was stronger than

he had imagined it could be, and he marvelled that it was a bond he'd been so set against forming.

But there was despair in him too and it cast a huge shadow over the joy.

Aislin hated him.

She was taking great strides and reclaiming her life for herself.

Whatever feelings she'd had for him had died. Dante had killed them.

The heavy dark raincloud that poured on him as he walked back to his car matched perfectly the dark heaviness in his heart.

The rose-gold engagement ring he'd brought with him burned a hole in his pocket.

Aislin opened the front door carefully and crept into the house.

'What are you sneaking about for?'

She jumped in fright, then laughed when Orla poked her head around the living room door.

'I wasn't sneaking. I was trying to be quiet in case you were asleep.'

'You think I can sleep when you're out on the road in this weather?'

It had been in weather like this that Orla had had her accident.

Aislin's late return to their home was because she had spent the day a three-and-a-half-hour drive away in Dublin at an interview with a publisher that specialised in historical tomes. She wasn't sure if it was for her, as she had told Orla in her message before she'd made the drive home, but it had felt good to get out of the house and away from her studies for a few hours.

Every time she looked at her textbooks she thought of Dante and remembered how he'd been thumbing through one of them when she had gone down the stairs in his cottage.

He'd couriered her luggage to her the day after she'd returned to Ireland.

Argh! She was thinking about him *again*.

Think only of the future. That was what she told herself constantly.

She kicked her boots off and forced a smile. 'Fancy a cup of tea?'

No matter how dreadful she felt inside, she would never let Orla know. Her sister felt bad enough about how Aislin had got the money for them without having to know the details of what had gone on between her and Dante.

It had broken her heart to tell her Dante didn't want to meet her or Finn. Orla had put a brave face on it but she'd been pretty cut up about his decision.

Tonight, however, Orla looked happier than Aislin had seen her in a long time.

'Has something happened?' Aislin asked as she walked into the poky kitchen.

'I would have told you earlier, but I wasn't sure how you'd react, and I didn't want to cause a distraction when you had such a long drive.'

She lifted the kettle. 'Tell me what?'

'We've had a visitor.'

She put the kettle under the tap. 'Oh?'

'Dante.'

The kettle slipped from her fingers and landed with a clang in the sink.

She composed herself quickly. 'Sorry. Butter fingers. He came?' She put it back under the tap and kept a tight grip on it.

'He did!' Orla's voice was full of joy.

Aislin busied herself with making the tea, letting her sister tell her all the details without interruption.

'He apologised for not wanting to see us. He needed time to process it, which is understandable. I mean, I've known about him for years, but my existence came as a bolt from the blue for him. He stayed for *ages*. Hours! I know you think he's a selfish cad, and that we should be grateful he doesn't want anything to do with us, but he's apologised for all that. I liked him very much.'

She pulled the mugs off the mug tree. Luckily Orla was so full of Dante's visit that she didn't notice the rattle Aislin made, bashing them together with her shaking hands.

'I'm glad he's shown a different side of himself to you,' she managed to say through a throat that felt as if a boulder had lodged in it. 'What did Finn think of him?'

'Finn adored him! He's promised him a new wheelchair for his birthday. I told him I was already planning one for the move but he insisted. He's coming to Finn's party.'

'Great.'

'He asked after you. Oh, I forgot to say, Dante's going to rent a house for us in Dublin until we can move into ours. He's going to arrange everything. We should be gone from here by the end of the week.'

'That soon?'

'Amazing, isn't it?'

She opened the fridge door and removed the milk. 'He's a quick mover.'

So quick he'd made her go from hating him to loving him in the space of a week…

The milk fell from her frozen fingers to the floor, the plastic bottle splitting on impact.

This time she was unable to compose herself.

She stared with horror at the milk spilling all over the floor and then looked into Orla's suddenly scared eyes. Eyes that were the image of Dante's.

'Ash?'

She clamped a hand to her mouth and shook her head.

Her heart pounded so hard she felt sick with the ripples. Panic tore at her throat.

Oh, dear God, she was in love with Dante.

What else explained the agony she had carried every minute of the thirteen days since she'd left Sicily?

Every night she went to bed and said a prayer for the pain in her heart to ease by the morning, but every morning she awoke after a fitful sleep with the pain a little worse.

Her appetite had gone to pot. She drank gallons of tea but could not stomach coffee because the mere smell of it reminded her of Dante.

Even looking at her own sister was painful because she could see the physical similarities between them.

Life had turned on its head for the better for the O'Reillys but Aislin had entered a living form of purgatory.

Orla read the despair on her sister's face, watched it crumble and watched her legs fall beneath her as she collapsed onto the wet floor, all of it happening as if in slow motion, and dived down to wrap her arms around her.

Aislin buried her face in her sister's comforting shoulder and, finally, the tears she'd held back for so long could no longer stay contained.

Orla stroked her back and her hair, trying her hardest to comfort her, letting her sister's hot tears soak through her jumper until there were no tears left to cry.

'Ash?' Orla stepped into the bedroom.

Aislin rolled over and rubbed the sleep from her eyes. Sunlight poured in through the thin curtains.

She must have slept for hours.

All that crying on Orla's shoulder and her overdue confession of her feelings for Dante had gone on until the early hours. The weight of it had exhausted her. She'd fallen asleep the moment her head had hit the pillow.

'What time is it?'

'Ten o'clock.'

So much for sleep being such a great healer. She still felt dreadful.

Sighing, she sat up as Orla perched on the bed beside her and held an envelope to her. 'This was delivered before I got up this morning.'

Aislin took the envelope with only her name scrawled on it. There was something lumpy and weighty in it.

She ripped it open.

A rose-gold pear-diamond ring fell onto the duvet.

Orla gasped.

Aislin could only stare at it as if it were something that could bite her.

'Is there a letter?'

Orla's voice cut through the roaring in her head.

She tried to breathe.

Fingers trembling, Aislin pulled out the note. She squeezed her eyes shut tightly.

Orla elbowed her ribs. 'Read it.'

'I'm scared,' she whispered.

'Read it.'

Filling her lungs, Aislin summoned the courage to open her eyes.

The writing was atrocious. The words, however…

*My darling Aislin,*

*This ring belongs to you to do with as you will.*

*I'm sorry for hurting you. I'm sorry for abusing your trust. I'm sorry for being a stubborn, distrustful fool. I'm sorry for everything. I hope one day you can find it in your heart to forgive me.*

*Thank you for taking such good care of our sister and nephew. Live your life for yourself now—I will be here always to share the load. I swear I will never hurt them again.*

*Whatever you decide to do with your life, be happy. You deserve happiness more than anyone I know.*

*My love for ever,*

*Dante x*

Aislin had to read the letter a dozen times before the words sank in.

*My love for ever...*

*My love for ever...*

*My love for ever...*

Her heart leapt, and with it she jumped off the bed and flew to her dressing table.

'What are you doing?' Orla asked, bemusement in her voice.

'Looking for my passport… Can you lend me some money?'

'No, but I can give you some.' Orla's grin went from ear to ear. 'Do you want me to book you a flight to Sicily while you get dressed?'

Dante carried the last box out to the corridor, laid it down for his men to take and put in the back of the truck with the other boxes, then stepped back into his father's office.

He was done.

He stared around at the empty space, bittersweet pain raging through him.

He'd flown back from Ireland early that morning knowing he had one more task to complete. He'd undertaken it alone. It had been the hardest job of his life.

The scent of cigars and bourbon had become very faint but he caught a trace and filled his lungs with the scent of his father one last time.

'I love you, Papa,' he whispered.

And then he turned the light out and closed the door of his father's office, knowing he would never step foot in it again.

The box had already been taken when Dante walked back down the corridor.

He didn't know what he was going to do with the house and the rest of its contents but this job was the one that had pressed on his shoulders with the greatest weight.

He checked the time as the flash of a vehicle's headlights passed the kitchen, his men taking the truck with the contents of his father's office.

Limbs heavy, he climbed the stairs to his childhood bedroom and sat on the bed that had been his for the first twenty years of his life.

Dante's football posters still hung on the walls. He nudged the bin with his foot and found the old ink stain he'd made on the carpet still there.

He looked out of the window at the huge back garden. His father had played football with him on that lawn. And rugby. And golf. Between them, they'd broken so many windows it had been impossible to keep count.

His mother was right—his father had been a wonderful father to him…

A tidal wave of grief punched him in the guts, doubling him over.

Sinking back onto the bed, he covered his face, unable to hold the tears back any longer.

He cried for the father he'd loved so much and who he missed with every fibre of his being.

And he cried for the woman he'd discarded as if she were a book to be thrown when he'd reached the last chapter.

She'd given him the chance of an epilogue. He saw that now. She'd jumped at the chance of extending their time together and he'd thrown it back in her face.

What a blind fool he'd been.

Aislin was moving on with her life and, other than their shared sister and nephew, that life did not involve him. He accepted that. But he'd been unable to leave Ireland without reaching out to her and letting her know how unbearably sorry he was.

The ring belonged to her. His heart did too. He had no one but himself to blame for her own heart despising him.

Through the crowding noise in his head he heard the faint chime of the doorbell.

Dante cradled his skull and took deep breaths.

He didn't want to see anyone. Not tonight.

Tonight he wanted nothing but to be left to grieve.

The bell rang again.

A moment later, a voice called out. 'Dante?'

He froze.

'Hello?' Aislin closed the door behind her and called out to him again. 'Dante?'

He *had* to be there. It felt like she'd searched the whole of Sicily looking for him. She'd started in Palermo, only to find he wasn't there and that none of his staff was prepared to tell her where he was; so she'd driven to the cottage, only to find it in darkness, covered in scaffolding and the doors locked. Back to Palermo she'd gone and this time she'd found Ciro. After much pleading, he'd given in and told her to try Salvatore Moncada's beachside villa.

'Aislin?'

She turned sharply to the sound of his voice and found him descending the stairs slowly, staring at her much like someone who'd seen a ghost.

For a long time she couldn't speak, only gaze at him. She soaked everything in. He looked…untamed. His hair was mussed, the beard he trimmed most days thick and bushy, his eyes bloodshot and puffy. He looked thinner too.

He reached the bottom of the stairs and stopped.

Slowly she stepped towards him, heart pounding, breath ragged, praying she hadn't misinterpreted the meaning behind his letter.

And if she had…

She had nothing to lose in being here. Nothing could be worse than the torture she'd lived through these past two weeks.

But she couldn't speak.

She cleared her throat and still the words wouldn't form.

He extended a hand and took a shuffling step towards her. His throat moved before he croaked, 'Why are you here?'

She cleared her throat again and finally managed to speak. 'I got your letter.'

He just stared at her.

Aislin took the deepest breath of her life. 'Dante… In your letter, you said whatever I do with my life I have to be happy. Dante… If I'm to be happy in my future…' Her voice became a whispered quiver, everything she wanted to say jumbled. 'The days I spent with you were the happiest I've ever known.'

'What are you saying?' he whispered.

A tear leaked down her cheek. 'That since I've left Sicily it's felt as if I don't know how to be happy any more. *You* make me happy.'

The eyes that hadn't left her face or even blinked gave a sudden spark of life.

'Dante, I'm sorry for the cruel things I said to you…'

*'No!'* Suddenly he was striding towards her, the warm hands whose touch she'd missed more than she'd believed humanly possible cupping her cheeks, fingers

kneading into her skin. 'Don't you dare apologise for speaking the truth. I behaved abominably.'

Dante cursed and gritted his teeth, sliding his hands around her face to delve his fingers into the russet hair he adored so much.

He'd thought he'd hallucinated her. But she was here, beautiful and sweet-smelling and solidly *real*.

He pressed his forehead to hers. 'I was scared… My feelings for you, all the things I was trying to deal with… I *couldn't* deal with any of it. I was a fool. The biggest fool. I told myself you were everything I didn't want when the truth is you are everything I need.'

Her glistening eyes widened and her chin wobbled.

He kissed her gently. 'I've known you such a short time but it feels as if you've been in my heart for ever.'

'You're in my heart too,' she whispered.

'Am I?' He hardly dared to believe… 'I thought you hated me.'

She placed a tender hand to his cheek and brushed her lips to his. 'I told myself I hated you because it was the only way I could cope, but the truth is I'm lost without you. I try to smile and plan for the future but it's all been a lie because I can't eat, I can't sleep… Our time together did something to me. *You've* done something to me. The only future my heart wants is a future with you.'

Suddenly he did dare to believe.

Dante dared to believe that his future could be happy too.

Claiming her mouth with his, he hauled her to him and wrapped his arms tightly around her, kissing the raspberry lips until he had no air left in him.

Breaking away to trace his mouth over her cheeks,

he then buried his nose into her hair and filled his lungs with her wonderful scent.

'I love you,' he whispered.

She nuzzled her nose into his neck. 'I love you too.'

Those four short words were sweeter than the sweetest confectionery. The weight that had compressed him since she'd gone not only lifted from his chest but from his entire body.

His heart beat loud and rapidly, but for the first time in weeks he could *breathe*, and the air he inhaled had never smelled so good.

When he next looked at the beautiful face he had missed so much, her smile infused every cell in his body with the sunlight it had missed without her. Dante made a vow to himself there and then that he would never drive her sunlight from his life again.

It was a vow he kept for the rest of his life.

# EPILOGUE

THE CATHEDRAL BOUNCED with the beams of the late-summer sun and, as Aislin approached it, careful of the enormous train of her dress which Orla and Sabine's children held with such care, and with her father's arm to hold on to, she thought back to the first wedding she'd attended in this great baroque building. Looking back, that was the day she had given her heart to Dante, and now here they were, four months later, about to exchange their own vows.

Dante had proposed to her on Finn's birthday. She hadn't had a moment's hesitation in saying yes. The beautiful rose-gold pear-diamond ring had been worn on her finger ever since. She would never remove it again.

He'd moved just as fast in getting her pregnant. Two days after she'd completed her degree, Aislin had taken the pregnancy test. Dante had squeezed her so tightly she'd almost choked.

The man who hadn't wanted anything to do with family had now decided he quite fancied having a football team of children.

Aislin thought a netball team might be more manageable.

Not even Orla's refusal to move to Sicily, despite

Dante's offer to buy her a home there, could mar her happiness. Modern technology and having Dante's private jet on tap meant they could be as involved in each other's lives as they'd always been. The round-the-clock care Dante had arranged for Finn meant Aislin could sleep knowing her beloved sister and nephew were both as well as they could be.

Aislin missed their daily presence but with Dante she had found something else—a piece of her soul.

He completed her. And, when she walked down the long aisle and saw the love reflecting in his eyes, she knew she completed him too.

Together they were the perfect fit.

Together they'd created their own heaven.

* * * * *

COMING NEXT MONTH FROM

HARLEQUIN Presents®

Available February 19, 2019

## #3697 THE SHEIKH'S SECRET BABY

*Secret Heirs of Billionaires*

by Sharon Kendrick

Sheikh Zuhal is shocked to discover he has a son! To claim his child, he must get former lover Jazz down the palace aisle. And he's not above using seduction to make her his wife!

## #3698 CLAIMED FOR THE GREEK'S CHILD

*The Winners' Circle*

by Pippa Roscoe

To secure his shock heir, Dimitri must make Anna his wife. But the only thing harder than convincing Anna to be his convenient bride is trying to ignore their red-hot attraction!

## #3699 CROWN PRINCE'S BOUGHT BRIDE

*Conveniently Wed!*

by Maya Blake

To resolve the royal scandal unintentionally triggered by Maddie, Prince Remi makes her his queen! But his innocent new bride awakens a passion he'd thought long buried. And suddenly, their arrangement feels anything but convenient...

## #3700 HEIRESS'S PREGNANCY SCANDAL

*One Night With Consequences*

by Julia James

Francesca is completely swept away by her desire for Italian tycoon Nic! But she believes their relationship can only be temporary—she must return to her aristocratic life. Until she learns she's pregnant with the billionaire's baby!

HPCNM0219RA

#3701 A VIRGIN TO REDEEM THE BILLIONAIRE
by Dani Collins

Billionaire Kaine has just given Gisella a shocking ultimatum: use her spotless reputation to save his own or he'll ruin her family for betraying him! But uncovering sweet Gisella's virginity makes Kaine want her for so much more than revenge...

#3702 CONTRACTED FOR THE SPANIARD'S HEIR
by Cathy Williams

Left to care for his orphaned godson, Luca is completely out of his depth! Until he meets bubbly, innocent Ellie. Contracting her to look after the young child is easy—denying their fierce attraction is infinitely more challenging...

#3703 A WEDDING AT THE ITALIAN'S DEMAND
by Kim Lawrence

To claim his orphaned nephew, Ivo needs to convince the child's legal guardian, Flora, to wear his ring. But whisking Flora to Tuscany as his fake fiancée comes with a complication...their undeniable chemistry!

#3704 SEDUCING HIS CONVENIENT INNOCENT
by Rachael Thomas

Lysandros has never stopped wanting Rio! A fake engagement to please his family is the perfect opportunity to uncover why she walked away... But Rio's heartbreaking revelation changes the stakes. Now he wants to give her everything...

*Ruthless billionaire Kaine has just given Gisella a shocking ultimatum: use her spotless reputation to save his own or he'll ruin her family for betraying him! But uncovering sweet Gisella's virginity makes Kaine want her for so much more than revenge...*

*Read on for a sneak preview of Dani Collins's next story,* A Virgin to Redeem the Billionaire.

"I went to the auction for an earring. I kissed a man who interested me. I've since realized what a mistake that was."

"It was," Kaine agreed. "A big one." He picked up his drink again, adding in a smooth, lethal tone, "I have half a mind to accept Rohan's latest offer just to punish you."

"Don't," Gisella said through gritted teeth, telling herself she shouldn't be shocked at how vindictive and ruthless he was. She'd already seen him in action.

He smirked. "It's amazing how quickly that little sparkler brings you to heel. I'm starting to think it has a Cold War spy transmitter in it that's still active."

"I'm starting to think this sounds like extortion. Why are you being so heavy-handed?"

"So that you understand all that's at stake as we discuss terms."

She shifted, uncomfortable, and folded her arms. "What exactly are you asking me to do, then?"

"You're adorable. I'm not asking. I'm telling you that, starting now, you're going to portray yourself as my latest and most smitten lover." He savored that pronouncement with a sip of wine that he seemed to roll around on his tongue.

"Oh, so you blackmail women into your bed."

For a moment, he didn't move. Neither did she, fearing she'd gone too far. But did he hear himself? As the silence stretched on, she began to feel hemmed in and trapped. Far too close to him. Suffocated.

"The fact you didn't hear the word *portray* says more about your desires than mine," he mocked softly. He was full out laughing in silence at her. So overbearing.

"I won't be blackmailed into playing pretend, either," she stated. "Why would you even want me to?"

He sobered. "If I'm being accused of trying to cheat investors, I want it known that I wasn't acting alone. I'm firmly in bed with the Barsi family."

"No. We can't let people believe we had anything to do with someone accused of fraud." It had taken three generations of honest business to build Barsi on Fifth into its current, iconic status. Rumors of imitations and deceit could tear it down overnight.

"I can't let my reputation deteriorate while I wait for your cousin to reappear and explain himself," Kaine said in an uncompromising tone. "Especially if that explanation still leaves me looking like the one who orchestrated the fraud. I need to start rebuilding my name. And I want an inside track on your family while I do it, keeping an eye on every move you and your family make, especially as it pertains to my interests. If you really believe your cousin is innocent, you'll want to limit the damage he's caused me. Because I make a terrible enemy."

"I've noticed," she bit out.

"Then we have an agreement."